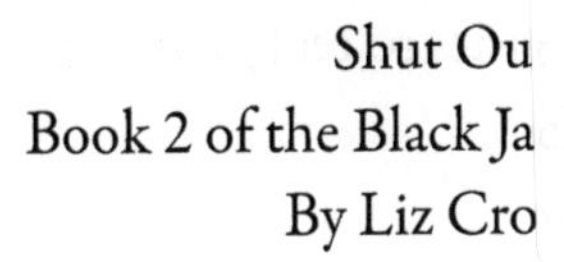

Shut Ou

Book 2 of the Black Jack Gentlemen

By Liz Cro

SHUT OUT

First edition. May 6, 2024.

ISBN: 979-8224817689

Written by Liz Crowe.

Part One

Chapter One

Sophie kept her chair turned from the office door, unwilling to even acknowledge the next soccer player awaiting her. She was sweaty and exhausted, with a blinding afternoon low-caffeine headache. Talking these over-paid, over-sexed, full-of-themselves prima donnas through their final contracts and benefits packages didn't help one bit. However, as head of legal for the team in its third year, she had a new crop of new players to orient—ten, to be exact.

But if one more of them waltzed in, reeking of sweat and staring at her as if she were the last crumb on the cookie tray, their flirty high beams blazing—so help her. As if she'd ever be interested in any of their little boy preening. For the thousandth time, she questioned her sanity, taking on this utter crapshoot of a project.

She closed her eyes a moment, shutting down her natural reaction to ponder the reasons, poke at them, rip off the scab that had more or less healed over them in her desperate attempt to start over.

"Hey," a deep, syrupy-sounding voice intoned, sending a strange tremor straight down her spine. "Um, am I in the right place?" It hit her ears as: 'm ah in the raht playce?

She swiveled around and shoved her glasses up her nose to get a good look at the next player looming in her doorway, taking in his jet-black hair, the strong lines of his stubbled jaw, and the breadth of his T-shirt clad shoulders. The Black Jack Gentlemen wore gray when they practiced, their uniforms provided by a famous shoe company, its logo emblazoned across the front. And said shirt clung to the sculptured torso blocking her doorway in a way that ought to be outlawed. All the while, Mr. Southern Accent stood stock still, as if used to being so frankly appraised.

A drop of sweat formed at her temple. She resisted the urge to wipe it away. He cleared his throat, so she jerked her gaze up to a set of the darkest eyes she had ever encountered. He smiled—a sweet, lopsided thing that imprinted itself on her brain in a wholly annoying way.

"Hey... uh... I'm Brody. Brody Vaughn." He ran fingers through his hair, nervousness as bright as a neon sign over his head.

Adorable. Her radar pinged like mad. But she forced it to shut the hell up. She had no business thinking about these kids in any way other than purely professional.

So far, they had all been the exact same breed of cocky assholes, alternating between eye-fucking her and extreme boredom in response to her monotonous drone of legalese. Sexy Southern Accent—"Brody," she muttered under her breath—put his hand out, as if to shake hers. His face reddened charmingly when she raised an eyebrow at his outstretched palm—the same one he'd just dragged through his sweat-soaked hair.

She rose slowly to her feet, needing to be at his level. He blinked, then dropped into the chair opposite hers without a word. Sophie took a long, calming breath, forcing herself to focus in ways she had learned, practiced, utilized in her years as a professional Dominatrix.

As she shut the door, keeping her back to the boy—to Brody who was not a boy, but a man—her pulse continued to race. Her heart pounded out its disconcerting rhythm, no matter what tricks she employed, which pissed her off. And that, finally, calmed her enough to face him.

"Hello, Mr. Vaughn. I'm Sophie Harrison, legal counsel for the Black Jack Gentlemen. I'll be explaining the terms of the contract you or your agent negotiated with our organization." She talked, using words she'd said a hundred times already. But her own voice echoed around in her head. She focused on the paper in front of her, irritated by her glasses, which kept sliding down her nose. All the while ignoring the raw, visceral reaction her body and brain were having to the man across from her—Brody, a twenty-six-year-old man, his player fact sheet stated.

No, he is a boy, and you don't play with boys. Not anymore.

She compressed her lips, pretending to find a nonexistent problem with the stack of legal documents pertaining to his agreement. To his credit, he stayed silent and still, in a way that intrigued her.

Finally, she met his gaze once more and blinked, then frowned. "So, another goalkeeper?" she asked, fully aware how it would needle the average, ego-driven, high-level athlete. A glimpse at his salary indicated his golden-child status. So this was the keeper the club had managed to sign, thanks to the aggressive recruiting activity by their assistant coach.

She tried out a casual smirk but discarded it. The way he looked at her as if memorizing her brought a hot flush to her cheeks. Straightening, she sucked in a breath and forced her thoughts to her next real workout—the kind she preferred that involved tight leather, her favorite bullwhip and a willing submissive.

"You okay there, Miz Harrison?" His voice slithered around in her brain, nestling in nice and low, gripping the base of her skull and making her want to jump up and run out of the room. She glared at him.

"I am fine." After shoving her glasses back up her nose, she slapped the contracts down in front of him, probably a little too hard. She needed Mr. Brody Vaughn the hell out of her office. She attempted to use her neutral face, to not snarl or growl or snap the poor kid's head off.

He shifted in his seat, cleared his throat, and glanced down at the papers she'd pinned under her manicured fingers, giving her a rush of control over the situation. Her spine tingled in a familiar way, but she channeled it, recognizing the distinct, loose, fluid feeling of compulsion.

"Now, let's go through this." She glanced down at her desk. His hand covered hers. Surprised, she flinched, and a strange, embarrassing sound emerged from her throat.

"I think you need a drink of water. You seem a little done in." His deep drawl coated her nerves like the sweetest honey-infused bourbon.

She snatched her water bottle, gulped some, and took a breath. Within thirty minutes she had laid out the terms of the contract, including his non-disclosure and good-behavior clauses, the health insurance guarantees, all of it. These players all had highly paid agents who'd likely been over it with him, but she wanted to do it to, to ensure there were no misunderstandings.

He asked a few questions, his voice soft, musical, and soothing in a way that had the opposite effect on her nerves. She gritted her teeth against the urge to lock the door and yank the kid's sweaty clothes off.

Jesus, help me. Get him out of here.

He rose quickly, startling her. "Well, if that's it."

She got to her feet, unwilling to look up at him at first and then noting how his chocolate brown eyes appeared to darken even further when she faced him.

"Yes. That will definitely be...ah... it." Wincing at her squeaky voice, she willed her knees to stop shaking. She would have little reason to encounter him again, unless he landed in trouble and she had to handle a legal problem on his behalf.

His physical presence, not that different from all the others who'd paraded through there in the last few days, compelled her in ways she refused to acknowledge. He stood nearly six-foot-six, which made sense, given his position on the team. His broad shoulders, narrow waist, long, strong legs, filled her brain.

He cleared his throat. And the traitorous flush crept up her neck to her face again. His angular features at that moment were set, and bored, perhaps a touch amused at her obvious discomfort. She narrowed her gaze. Why hadn't she noticed it before? Her pulse fluttered as she put a hand to her throat.

As if reading her mind, Brody Vaughn lifted his chin slightly, and she got a good look at the black chain imprinted at the base of his neck.

A dark, circular pattern of interlocking, heavy loops was inked onto tanned flesh. He smiled again, slow moving like his drawl, and touched it once, then turned, giving her a breathtaking rear view of the chain as he walked toward the office door.

The man wore a collar, a permanent one. But the vibes he threw her proclaimed one thing loud and clear. The person who'd bestowed the collar no longer had any claim on him.

Her mind swooped, whirled, and doubled around on itself, picturing him—Brody, the man—at her knees, bound, and awaiting her command. She shivered and jumped when her assistant appeared at the door. Brody had left, trailing that mysterious aura of vulnerability and strength behind him.

Chapter Two

"Vaughn! Where are you?"

Brody sat staring at his feet, ignoring the usual post-match noise and bustle around him. Reminders of how poorly he'd performed today were not going to help him. He'd been playing soccer in some capacity since he began walking, since he had memories of anything. And today had been among his worst performances, ever.

From the hills of East Tennessee, to the streets of Nashville, he'd been on teams, in clubs, trained by himself, trained by pros, the whole nine yards. He'd seen every sort of match condition. Every possible coaching style. Experienced all the officiating missteps and seen plenty of parental overreactions. He realized what it meant to suck serious ass. He'd done so today. And he understood why, too. Hence the dark clouds draping his consciousness.

The team manager drew closer, his deep voice joined by another, as a sort of bonus, really. Brody leaned against the dark wood lining the walls in the over-the-top, fancy locker room.

Metin Sevim, a Turk, had been a Spanish league phenom with the world at his feet when a horrific tragedy struck, leaving him drunk and useless for years. But he'd bounced back, had a family now, and was all-in-all a decent, if tough, coach. At that moment, he had a look on his face Brody Vaughn understood well enough. It was the we-lost-and-it's-pretty-much-your-fault glare that coaches the world over had perfected. That "saying it without actual words" expression players dreaded, regardless of what level of the game they played.

Exhausted in mind and spirit, sick of the chewing out before it even started, Brody gazed at the two men in front of him now. Rafael Inez, the team's manager, had snapping eyes that reflected the same displeasure as Metin's. He opened his mouth first, but the coach put a hand on his arm. The men regarded each other as the swirl of post-match activity came to a loud crescendo around them.

Players in various stages of undress wandered in and out of the main locker room, grabbing towels and pulling on the dress pants, shirts, and ties the club required of them when entering and leaving the facility mostly in silence. One thing Brody would say about the former-hot-headed, player-turned-failure-turned-coach, Metin knew when not to talk. He tilted his head, still pinning Brody with something that faded from this is your fault to what-the-hell-is-wrong-with-you.

Then he sighed and, to Brody's surprise, dropped onto the bench next to him, leaned forward, elbows on knees, and seemed to examine the rubberized floor. Brody hadn't even made it to the shower yet. He felt so weighed down and lethargic, lifting his arms took more energy than existed on the planet.

How could he even begin to describe what was wrong with him? Heart pounding, legs aching, his shoulder was screaming where he'd landed on it, hard, then waved away the trainer at the sixty-fifth minute. By that time, all the players were gassed from the late summer heat, but held on, toe-to-toe, with the Canadian national team in a friendly match. The stupid, sneaky forward had seen him wincing, favoring his left shoulder, and drove the ball straight in on his weakened side. It had been a simple fifty-fifty ball—face to face. He had blown it, him and his overpaid, lame ass, wobbly self.

Yeah. Thanks to his quick encounter with the front office legal woman, he'd been rendered a quivering, useless, uncertain heap of need. How in god's name could he explain that to his coaches?

"So," his coach said, his voice low, soft, and more ominous than if he were slamming shit around and calling Brody every foul name in the book. "You want to explain to me what happened? Because I have to tell you, Vaughn, that flat-footed, rookie-ass move on your part killed us. You know how Jackson works. He always goes left. We talked about this and you caught, what, four other tries? Then you miss one that he projected like a Sunday matinee?"

His coach's voice tightened, and Brody clenched his jaw. To his credit, the guy maintained his cool. Rafael started to speak, but Metin held up his palm again without tearing his gaze from Brody's face. The tension rose between the two coaches.

Great, now I'm gonna get caught in some kind of power play between these two? I gotta get out of here.

The whole scene was too confusing to tolerate. He leapt to his feet, skin crawling with nervous energy, and mumbled, "I need to take a shower." Used to coaches ripping, roaring, cursing, throwing, tearing, spitting, coming just short of actual physical abuse, this quiet, contemplative coach's question time made him nervous.

As the new kid—and the highest paid one on the team thanks to his razor-sharp agent—he'd lost the Black Jack Gentlemen's first friendly of the new season. The mental blackness kept coming, threatening and terrifying. He shouldn't have come there. He should have stayed behind in a second string goalkeeper slot and remained firmly ensconced in his comfort zone. He shouldn't have let his agent talk him into the stupid expansion team. And he definitely should have never walked into Sophie Harrison's office.

He waited for his coach and the team manager to say more, but they stayed silent. Figuring it some kind of reverse psychology bullshit, he shrugged, stripped out of his uniform, and stalked into the shower room.

Fuck them if they weren't going to coach him. He'd figure it out on his own.

Maybe.

The steam rolled around him, opening his sinuses, clearing his head a little. Although she remained there, lodged, nice and firm in his cerebellum.

He sighed, turned his face up to the water, and propped his hands on the tiled wall. Wound tight and probably out of her league in the soccer world, but dear god and sonny Jesus, she had legs that went on for miles, ending in a pair of sky-high leather boots. Her curves nipped into that soft, expensive gray suit, the jacket gaping just enough in the front for him to get a glimpse of the tops of her breasts.

Brody loved nothing more than putting his tongue to a woman's warm, pulsing neck, to touch her delicate collarbones. And Sophie, with her chestnut hair scraped into a severe bun, her huge, eyes like giant pools of ocean blue, had projected the thing he wanted so badly he had indeed fucked up this game today, because of his own weak, lame, uselessness.

"Shit!" He put his fist into the tile, barely feeling it as his body went on ultra-high alert, his brain clicking into a kind of autopilot, a space he hadn't inhabited in years. Not since his beloved Mistress had banished him from her bed, her dungeon, her life, because their professor-student affair had been exposed. She'd been afraid to jeopardize his last few months as a NCAA Division I scholarship soccer player—the year Vanderbilt men's soccer went all the way, defeating a favored Indiana team, 2-1.

Shivering, teeth chattering, he slid to the floor, ignoring the white-hot pain that permeated his shoulder. He groaned as his body hardened even further against his will, and water continued its relentless tattoo on his skin.

Chapter Three

Sophie tapped her teeth with the expensive Mont Blanc pen she'd kept, like a bizarre talisman, since passing the bar years before. It had anchored her through an amazing run of success, then a descent into madness, and her eventual emergence, more or less, to this limbo state.

She stared out the window onto the field—the pitch, she reminded herself. Her office boasted a perfect view of the giant stadium, like all the other executive spaces, a detail that had been emphasized repeatedly during the interview process when it became clear the club wanted her more than she wanted them.

As if I give a flying rat's patootie about this stupid game.

Narrowing her gaze at the sight of the men, she found herself mesmerized by them. Bunch of grossly overpaid, overgrown little boys going through their paces for the second time that day. She spotted all the new ones she'd met with to discuss the terms of their employment. Most of them she lumped together in a stew of chest-pounding testosterone, guys who'd been told since the day they were born that they were walking, talking gods among mortals. Being constantly told that by parents, siblings, coaches, fellow players, and mostly by women they bedded, it might start to feel like a home truth.

Her gaze drifted across their masses—the young, handsome captain who'd actually proven to be the one thing that tamed their wild card—the hot, Euro-trash player. Which had resulted in the two of them engaging in an open, gay male relationship. A topic of much debate and dissatisfaction in the marketing department since the coaching staff refused to allow them to be paraded about as an example of how forward-thinking the organization was. There was the sleek South African giant of a man who'd joked and put her at ease for a brief while during their meeting. Smiling, she put her fingers to her throat when she spotted the ginger-haired, quick-tempered Irish kid,

Nick. He'd eyeballed her for a split second, seemingly shocked that someone as feminine as she would inhabit the team's front office. Then he'd blushed and apologized, barely lifting his gaze to meet hers again, as if he didn't think he could manage it without staring at her boobs.

The Turkish coach and South American manager stalked the sidelines, gripping clipboards and computer tablets while observing the training session. Both men were tall, dark-skinned, and brutally attractive. How she had managed to emerge from her life's recent chaos in this sea of hot guys, literally surrounded by all this flaming testosterone, she had no earthly idea.

She frowned, seeking out the figure she wanted, the one her optic nerves seemed to crave like a PMS sufferer craves chocolate. Where was the goalkeeper? She rested her forehead against the cool glass, admiring the sleek, aggressive, yet dance-like movements of the men. Strong thighs flexed, bare arms gleamed with sweat, broad shoulders collided, as their fit, firm, bodies bounced off each other, and reconnected just for the sake of controlling a silly black and red orb—the sphere that determined their very existence in this space.

Then she spotted him. Brody Vaughn, the goalkeeper, nearly a full head taller than all of them, but for the South African. Dark hair cut short to his skull, almost military strict, his full lips at that moment split in a grin, his teeth flashing.

She sucked in a breath when he dropped to the turf and rolled onto his side, pulling first one knee, then the other, up to his chest. The stretching, flexing, and blatant exposure of his ass and thighs made her want to cry, to scream, to call out for him. She forced herself away from the eye candy. There was work to do, and she had a paying customer who required her undivided attention that evening.

The glare of sunlight distracted her. She cursed the office designers for the millionth time as she angled the blinds over and over again, forcing her to the window—and her gaze to the pitch. That was where Brody, the young man who had populated her every sleeping, overwrought moment since she'd met him, went through his paces like the well-paid show pony he was.

"Hey, Harrison."

She jumped at the sound of a deep, gravelly voice from behind her. She turned and smiled at the man filling the doorway. "Jack, to what do I owe this pleasure?" She walked around behind her desk, praying he hadn't caught her gawking at his high-paid stable of soccer studs. "You gracing us in the D for a reason?"

He glared down at a tablet screen, then flopped into one of her cushy chairs, heaving a teenager-worthy sigh. "I swear I had no idea these guys would be so...." He waved a hand, apparently unable to find the right word.

"Let's see," she said, holding fingers as she spoke. to count the ways. "Unbelievably immature? Childish? Needing a round-the-clock guard to stop them from fucking around and causing public relations nightmares?" she asked.

"Is there anything that requires my direct attention?" he asked.

They'd had their fair share of legal issues, from DUIs, a couple of drunk and disorderlies at strip clubs, a domestic dispute that ended up being a not-so-funny practical joke, and a paternity suit. All in a day's work, really. She had no complaints.

Her private cell phone buzzed from deep in the recesses of her large leather briefcase. Jack Gordon, the driving force behind the entire project, kept his eyes glued to the computer tablet he'd carried in, no doubt studying the profit-and-loss reports, something he obsessed over daily. Shifting in her seat, she reached into her purse and flipped the device over.

A message flashed from Lance, her business partner and security guard for her other job. Before she allowed frustration at her overworked schedule to enter her consciousness, Sophie visualized her bank account, slowly creeping toward its former robust state, thanks to the man sitting across from her who signed her paycheck, but also to her moonlighting work.

"Hey, you okay?"

She shot him what she hoped passed for a sincere look, shoved the mess of the past six years out of her head, and focused on her boss and their new list of legal issues. "Yes. I'm good. Now about these new players..."

• • • •

LATER, THEY SAT TOGETHER in one of the three brewpubs inside the giant, state-of-the-art stadium. Over beers and burgers, they finished up the lengthy list of various player, and some fan-induced, bullshit. At one point, Jack leaned back in his chair, stretching arms over his head.

"You seem out of sorts, favorite grossly overpaid attorney lady," he said, his voice easygoing.

She'd learned early on not to gloss over anything with him. He demanded straight forwardness from everyone. Thanks to his diligence and determination, the Black Jack Gentlemen, the expansion team that had been slated for Vegas, resided in the Motor City instead. The club had turned a profit and two winning seasons into the new soccer league's owners for consideration—the best record of any other expansion team.

"Yeah, okay. You're right." Between late nights and her growing, unhealthy obsession with the team's prize new goalkeeper, she was a mess. Something had to give.

Jack stayed silent. She restrained the urge to tell him to mind his own business. No, that bitchy Sophie Harrison, former partner in the Harrison and Winter patent-specialty law firm, had been squashed like a bug under the heel of fate.

Gazing into Jack Gordon's deep blue eyes, she pondered yet again the odd twist in the road that brought her here working for a man whose best friend had been the one guy she'd fallen for and shoved out of her life so hard, he'd taken her at face value and left. Her brief, intense relationship with Evan Adams had scared her, forced her to do and say things she didn't mean, which had in turn driven him away. Which had sent her straight into a downward spiral that ended with her submitting to a man who'd very nearly killed her, or at least almost ruined her.

"You need a break, Soph?" Jack asked, filling the awkward silence.

"No. That is the very last thing I need."

They both looked up at a loud clamor of voices, masculine laughter, and catcalls coming down the long, wide hallway toward them. They sat outside on the fake alfresco patio of the brew pub that was, ironically, an extension of Evan Adams' successful Big House Brewing venture in Ann Arbor. The place opened every day at eleven a.m. and did a brisk business from downtown office workers, artists, off-duty athletes, and others who peopled the recovering city.

Brody led the group, dressed in suit pants that hugged his ass and a dress shirt that wrapped his torso so perfectly Sophie had to clench her hands into fists under the table at the sight of it. They had indeed managed to avoid each other as she predicted that first day, but for the times he would do this whole running into her thing as she ate, or ran laps around the large stadium pitch, trying to find some alone time with her thoughts.

His full lips curved up, that crooked smile seeming to mock, but at the same time placate her. He continued to move toward them, hypnotizing her, stopping right at the table where she sat with the man who'd launched the entire so-far-successful venture. Then he winked at her—winked!—like a flirtatious school kid.

Her skin flushed hot. She frowned at him. When she met Jack's gaze again, he had an eyebrow raised. Finally, the players wandered off, still laughing, joking, and talking over each other.

"I hear our expensive new goal keeper has a new girlfriend," Jack said, making her freeze with anxiety. Had she been that obvious?

"I don't know why you think I would care."

Jack shrugged, finished his beer, and stood. She remained in her seat, not quite ready to trust her knees to support her.

"Watch yourself." He grinned then walked away, taking a call and already on to something else, leaving her alone and filled with lust, fury, and frustration.

Chapter Four

Brody watched the woman's thin frame coming toward him. He felt detached, as if he were watching some other guy look at a woman. A woman without a stitch of clothing, who was firm and tanned with big breasts out of proportion to her narrow hips. The line of abdominal muscles, just obvious enough to prove that the body's owner committed a lot of time and energy to making them that way, drew his gaze lower, taking in the protruding hip bones and lower still.

Biting his tongue to keep from asking why she waxed herself that way, making her body resemble that of a pre-adolescent girl, he took her in his arms. Even though his brain refused to engage.

Her lips parted, revealing teeth that were honest-to-god blinding white. Her small nose was ever so slightly upturned in a calculated-to-be-cute way. Noises came from her throat that shocked him, until he realized that it was because of him, of what he was doing with his fingers while his other hand stroked her face, then cupped one obnoxiously full breast and brushed at a nipple.

She smelled of soap and shampoo, tasted of toothpaste, as if she wished to disguise anything resembling a natural or normal human odor or flavor. Her body molded against his equally naked form. A cold palm gripped his dick, and his mind clicked in for a second at the sensation. The noises continued pouring out of her. He heard his name, the name of the Lord, moans, groans, affirmations. At the last moment, he pushed her back, rolled on a rubber and crawled between her legs. The in-and-out motions that followed were boring and mechanical.

The girl beneath him writhed, holding onto his hips with her long, spinning-class-strong legs, her overpowering perfume filling his nose. Hormones rushed into his brain, giving it a long, loving hug. He shuddered and a noise burst from his lips as he experienced yet another orgasm after little effort, which he hated. He felt weak for allowing it.

The girl kept her legs fastened tight around his waist, her arms around his neck, and her minty-fresh breath hot in his ear. He wanted to scream with frustration and unhappiness. All things a man shouldn't feel after coming as hard as he just had.

"Baby," she cooed, finally releasing him after he waited her out, trying not to leap up and run out of his own condo to escape her.

Brody rolled onto his back and draped an arm across his face, willing her to disappear, to go poof and be gone, leaving behind a vague scent of soap.

She did the opposite, draping her perfect limbs over his. She made annoying sounds as she ran her red, manicured fingernails over his slightly sweaty chest. Sleep threatened, as it always did, thanks to the natural activity occurring in his brain and bloodstream. But he fought it off, slipped out from under the tangle of female limbs, and sat, gripping the edge of his bed, staring at the expensive carpet at his feet.

He hated himself and his well-known need to be around people all the time, to never be left alone. It had led him to this very post-coital moment with the daughter of a wealthy local plastic surgeon. She'd spotted Brody at some fundraiser the team had been forced to attend, in full monkey-suited glory, in the Detroit Institute of the Arts about a month ago. Her determined beeline for him had been unavoidable. She'd dragged him around for a while, spouting her art knowledge while he'd pondered his options.

He'd been lonely, so he'd caved, taken her up on her unspoken offer, bought her a few drinks at a club, then taken her to his condo and fucked her silly. Now, attached like a goddamned barnacle, she wouldn't release him no matter how rude he tried to be, how asshole-ish his behavior, how many times he ignored her calls and texts, only to have her show up, ripe and ready for his taking at the drop of a hat.

A WAG...or better, a WOG, Wife or Girlfriend of almost-famous athlete Brody Vaughn, the highly touted goalkeeper for the team to watch, was exactly what and where she wanted to be. She... oh shit, what is her name? He winced when she draped herself over his shoulders, kissing his neck and muttering about a party at Daddy's house.

He rose, forcing her to slide off him. Shivering, he pulled off the condom and slammed the bathroom door behind him, then stared in the large mirror, face red, mind swirling. She moved around, making rustling noises he sincerely hoped were her clothes, covering up the expensively toned and perfect body.

Goddamn, son, you are lame—she is prime, and yours for the taking. Of course, it would help if you could remember her name.

He splashed water on his face again and again. His balls tingled. His neck ached. His shoulder sang out with familiar pain. He had soreness in nearly every nook and cranny of his body. But he wanted more. No, he craved more. Something no vanilla-scented, buffed-out, over-tanned, wanna-be-wife could provide.

Ugh. You sound worse than all those mouth-breathing assholes in the locker room, with their jokes and shitty things they'd say about the women in their lives.

Gasping, he slid to the floor and gripped his knees, shaking so hard his teeth rattled. Images shot through his brain. He pressed his hands to his temples, willing them away. Still they advanced, inexorable, grinning at him and dragging him back into the hell he'd escaped as a boy, after his single mother died of a drug overdose and he'd been forced through the system. Which translated to multiple foster homes in ten years until landing on his own two feet at eighteen with an academic and soccer scholarship to one of the South's most exclusive universities. This after ten years spent sleeping on couches, in basements and spare rooms, never actually accepted into anything like a normal family, merely a paycheck for whatever adult he'd been assigned to for the time being.

The two things he had going for him, his brain and his soccer skills, kept him alive and sane, focused on his future. The last place he'd lived while finishing high school in a barely there town in Southeast Kentucky had something resembling a real soccer coach. A guy who'd played in college and returned home to teach and coach. He'd been the reason Brody escaped with a full ride to Vanderbilt University.

Those years were ones he refused to visit, even in his loneliest, most fevered moments when his body and brain craved the discipline, the pain, the ropes, the metal, and the leather that freed him, allowed him to be what he was, if for a fleeting moment. Until he'd become this shameless sports man-whore, ripe for the picking, who'd been plucked by the nameless girl now whaling on the bathroom door.

"Hey, Brody," she whined, her voice like a full chorus of fingernails scraping slowly down a wall of chalkboards. "What're you doing in there? I need to go. But I'll see you tonight? At Daddy's? At the club? Okay? Baby?"

Kelli. With-an-i—yeah. Of course.

"Yeah. Whatever. Bye," he grunted out. Any sane woman with a sense of pride would tell him to go fuck himself and never show up again. Yeah. Kelli had a different set of priorities. Sighing, he waited for the inevitable.

"Okay, baby. So good to see you again. Love you bunches. Call me!"

Oh, god. He had to get out of this, fast—before the temptation to drive his car into a concrete wall took hold for real.

Chapter Five

Sophie stepped back, observing her work for the night. The familiar handle of the bullwhip lodged tight in her palm. A sheen of sweat cooled her as a breeze parted the curtains. Moonlight streaked across the dark hardwood floor, crossing the man's bare, whip-striped torso. Distracted, she gazed out over the city, its huge, hulking, mostly empty buildings, barren streets, and no-man's-land vibe, ignoring her client, who was strapped to a large X-shaped cross.

The city had once been such a jewel, a thriving hub on the edge of Canada, gleaming and glamorous with its French-inspired architecture and multi-culture. When the 1960s roared in, bringing race riots and fury, it left an empty husk in its wake, an echoing reminder of what was, and what never would be again for reasons bemoaned by plenty, but dealt with by none. Her own life mirrored it. Probably why she had such an affinity for it and what kept her here.

Continuing to ignore her client, she rubbed the end of the whip's handle along her neck and across the top of her exposed breasts, deep in thought. She'd come from a background of privilege. Had a fully functional and supportive family. Her parents had loved her, their Sophie, the beautiful, desired only child of a pair of college professors mired in their own self-importance. Their one flaw was over-involvement in her life from her conception. Their near constant presence was taken from her in the blink of an eye, in an auto accident, while she finished law school in Ann Arbor. She missed them, but sometimes worried that she didn't miss them enough.

She'd never been close to anyone, not her parents or her friends in high school and college. No one made an impact on her as she worked toward her goal. To have her own law firm, her own money, to live the way she wanted.

Hard, brittle, and bitchy had been the name of her game then. How she had gotten to that point escaped her, but it represented a stage of her life and she'd done little to dispel the image. It might be a self-created perception, but she liked that everyone considered her in control of everyone and everything around her.

Then, just when she believed she had crafted the perfect balance of work and play, he had dropped into her life, landing in her lap like a Christmas present you didn't know you wanted and can't accept.

Her goals had been simple. She'd achieved them, thanks to her own doing. Had even found an outlet for her restlessness—the never-quite-satisfied, high-level lust she sustained nearly around the clock. But Evan Adams had upset that apple cart, sending her into a strange free fall of unwanted emotion.

Shaking her head, she turned her body on autopilot, needing to finish this guy off and get some sleep. She fixed her Dominatrix voice in place, and flicked her whip at the man, who flinched and moaned around his ball gag. A tough one, this guy. An M.D. CEO at a major medical center who loved nothing more than harsh treatment of his entire body: nipple clamps, cock rings, restraints galore, gags, blindfolds, the works. She drew the line at the asphyxiation play, though, unwilling to even contemplate it.

Tonight, he had dropped to his knees in his suit at the sight of her, dressed in thigh-high, stiletto-heeled boots, thong panties, and nothing else. Her high powered client was a breast man. Part of their deal was that she never covered hers during his sessions.

Such was her five-hundred-dollar-an-hour life as a professional Dominatrix. A cash-only business, the side career had helped her rebuild her finances and her psyche—both of which were decimated by a guy she had come within a month of marrying.

She smiled, noting the good doctor's pleasant, heavy erection that he'd maintained for nearly four hours. Once she hit the two thousand dollar moment, she let him come. He never failed to impress her with his restraint.

Tonight, however, she required something more. Something they had agreed upon at their first meeting they would deal with on an as needed basis.

Having done her research, she understood she skirted the edges of illegality, but for one small detail. Actual sex, the insertion of a man's penis into her vagina, was forbidden unless she demanded it. If she wanted it, she would give a simple command and the deed would be accomplished.

She had only done so once, in the early days, when she still attached some emotion to the act. Since then she'd gone without and done her whipping, caning, flogging, wax-dripping, ball-gagging, cock-ringing, restraining, and orgasm-inducing thing from a distance.

Ripping off his blindfold, she sprang his wrists free and put her leather-gloved palm to his handsome, if somewhat mottled, face.

"Fuck me, slave," she hissed into his ear.

He did as he was told.

Later, after the money exchange, the good doctor was sliding his arms into his suit coat when he spoke. "You know I'm married, right?"

She glanced up from where she slumped, body languid from a decent orgasm, a stack of one-hundred-dollar bills piled neatly on the table next to her. The laugh burst out of her before she was able to stop it, drag it back, and avoid the inevitable. Rising to her feet, still clad in the ridiculous boots, she pointed to the door.

"We're done. Don't call me again."

His face lost its superiority in one fell swoop. Which brought more laughter bubbling up. Men. So transparent. "Just because I want you to use that cock to get me off, you honestly think I want anything more from you than that... or this?"

She put her hand on the money, heart pounding with fury and something else, something she refused to acknowledge lest she burst into embarrassing tears. She forced herself to keep her voice calm, low, and firm. "Get the hell out. Don't call me again until you're ready to do what I say without assuming anything about me. Do you understand?"

Grabbing the whip, she snapped it in his direction. Her client groaned as the crotch of his dress pants swelled, as always. This guy really had some issues, but she liked him. If she were a different woman, with different priorities, she might make a play for him.

"I said get out."

He gulped, started to speak, then slipped out the door. She dropped back into her chair and burst into surprising and unwelcome tears.

Chapter Six

Brody wiped the sweat from his eyes and focused on the guy bearing down on him, the ball at his feet. He kept his gaze locked on the black and red sphere, the way he'd been trained, observing the man's legs, watching his hips turn slightly to the right, forcing Brody to adjust his tactic at the last minute. The ball the star forward on the Orlando team had been prepared to plant right in the back of his net landed neatly in his arms. The crowd roared. Brody winked at the guy.

"Not in my house," he said, putting all he had behind a kick, sending the ball sailing over the heads of both teams. His team's first striker spent about four seconds getting it between the legs of his opposite, the flat-footed keeper in the other goal.

God, I love this game.

Something seemed to be going right for a change. He seemed to have his soccer act together, anyway. The match ended in a one-all draw. Which led to the sort of ending every decent goalkeeper craved—the shoot out. He downed some water, poured the rest over his head, and glared at the line of asshole opposing players who honestly thought they would get a shot past him.

Shaking out his arms, he rolled his shoulders, took a few quick breaths, and crouched, never more ready. The first kick went wild to the left, not coming near the net. He stayed completely still, which always unnerved the kicker. The second one hit him square in the chest. He laughed and tossed it back out. The third shot forced him to take a diving leap to the left, but he saved it from entering his protected territory.

He got a breather when the other goalie had to go to work. His team made one point off their turn, taking a bit of pressure off him. He smacked his gloved hands together, rolled his sore shoulder, and winked at the pipsqueak about to kick. He stopped all three attempts with little effort.

His team then scored twice, and the match ended. He dropped to his knees as all the positive energy whooshed out of him in a scary rush. His head pounded and his hands shook. The game was over. He had to leave the field, the one place he wanted to be. He now had to get showered, get dressed in his suit, and go to some god-awful event. with... whatshername... Kelli. Yeah. Kelli's daddy was hosting a fundraiser, and he'd promised to attend. He tried hard not to puke.

He shot a weak smile to his celebrating teammates, got to his feet and trudged off the pitch without a word to anyone. Maintaining his silence as if encased in a cocoon, he cleaned up, got dressed, and stuck his sunglasses on his head, ignoring all the whooping and hollering going on around him as he headed toward the door.

A few players slapped him on the ass, yelled various profanities. But Brody's vision tunneled as he flipped his internal switch over to autopilot, biting back a yell of frustration.

He'd been a goalkeeper for the last six of ten years playing the game. It had proven a naturally isolated place as the eyes on the field, part of the team, but at the same time the ultimate loner. The guy who had the final say. The place where the proverbial buck stopped. And he was most at home there, simultaneously in the group but set apart.

A hand dropped on his shoulder, startling him out of his semi-trance.

"Great saves, Vaughn," his coach said. Brody stared at him about a half-second too long for his silence to be polite. "You're in a hurry. Headed to the Grosse Pointe thing tonight?"

He tried and failed to suppress a shudder. Metin stared at him, his hand still on a shoulder that suddenly ached like a bitch as a reminder that he'd forgone the usual post-game therapy of massage and ice.

I am losing my ever-loving mind.

"Uh, yeah, I am."

He stepped out of Metin's reach, something the coach noted and Brody understood he noted. His skin crawled as if an army of ants was marching over every inch of him. Trying hard not to recall what he'd done to relax after stressful college games, he gulped, willed his body not to react to the memory as he pasted on a weak smile.

He wanted to be forced into a place in his head that he missed so badly it kept him awake at night. But instead, by way of avoiding conflict, he was going to one of Kelli's father's many fundraisers. For the hundredth time, he honestly wondered how he had gotten here.

Just as his coach started to speak, no doubt to impart some bit of wisdom or advice Brody wouldn't take even if he wanted to, a shout and loud bang distracted him. Metin blinked and suddenly the noise of whatever the hell had happened around the corner of lockers got louder.

"See you there," he mouthed, before turning and yelling at the players, who sounded as if they had decided that a Greco-Roman wrestling match was a good use of their celebration energy.

"Yeah, sure," Brody said to his retreating back. He stood for a minute, listened to Metin curse and separate the idiots. Unbidden, a vision so clear and bright he hoped the whole locker room couldn't see it, appeared before him.

It was She, his Mistress. Her thick red hair, long, slim legs, full lush lips, possessed of his peace, his everything, burned before him. The last time he'd seen her, the night the text hit both their phones with the blackmail threat, she'd been in rare form. Just before the final game of the NCAA Final Four men's soccer game, he'd been a head case, a total wreck with the sort of pulsing, pounding nervousness that only high-level athletes, actors, dancers, rock stars, or concert pianists can ever truly appreciate.

He knew why he had these visions. Because his entire soul craved her and how She and only She could bring him down off the high from a match. He needed it, she convinced him. And he'd been programmed to play to the best of his ability, to shower, and go straight to Her.

His Mistress understood and trained him well. She'd take one look at him when he arrived at her front door before yanking him inside, tossing him to the floor as if he weren't a six-foot-six, semi-professional athlete, and she a petite woman twenty years his senior.

She would strip off his clothes, her low, sexy voice whispering, then yelling her commands. She liked to truss him up, use the well-worn soft cotton ropes against his skin. He loved to fight them, shifting around for the express purpose of hearing them creak. And the sweet, sharp bite of the whip always soothed his freshly showered skin.

Within an hour, he'd be a weeping mess. The hour after that, relaxed and finally at peace, having given up the natural testosterone-fueled tendency of a strong, virile male to fight back and resist her. Which reflected the beauty of his psyche. That much he had learned at Her hand after years of wholly unsatisfactory sex with various women. He required the pain, the submission, and the commands. And then, more from the bullwhips, or better yet, the hard wooden cane.

She wielded candle wax, ice cubes, and clamps like no other. Nothing helped settle his mind more than focusing on the very real pain she brought, preferably while his wrists and ankles were shackled with metal or silk or cotton.

He had exquisite control over his own orgasm after all this training. Able to approach the very brink of release, only to slink away, so he could keep going. She always took her pleasure first, sometimes denying him for an entire night while she came over and over again.

But this woman he'd allowed himself to touch, to finger, to fuck, she had the opposite effect. Kelli-with-an-i made him come fast and hard, like a goddamned kid, and afterward he felt even more overwrought. He wanted that control back. But had no idea how to regain it.

His legs shook so hard he had to drop to the large wooden bench that stretched along the wall in front of somebody's locker. That last night had imprinted on him, tattooed like one of the inked messages or images on his skin. He touched his neck, sensing the chain he'd had done for Her. It seemed hotter than the surrounding skin, in a sort of sympathetic agony.

"Go, Brody,'" she'd yelled at him, her huge green eyes snapping. He was unbound and set loose, naked, and he had no idea what to do or say. "You have to. We're done. I release you. I command you to leave me." She was loud and a little screechy with panic.

He understood it now. But at that moment, he'd wanted to jump off a bridge, seeing her angry, panicked face as she screamed at him to get out of her life.

The rest of the scene blacked out like a television with the power cut. He stood, dropped his sunglasses into place, unwilling to revisit the abject horror of it. Not to mention the following days when his entire life imploded while he watched, helpless to do anything about it.

The next day, Vanderbilt had won the men's soccer championship, a first in their program's history. Brody had saved the day in the eighty-sixth minute when it seemed Indiana would rebound from a missed corner kick. He lunged right, nearly missing the ball, then stuck his leg out as if on autopilot, and kicked it free of the net. They had won 1-0. Thanks to photos and sports news reports, he got to experience it later. But recalled none of it as it happened. All he knew was that he had been rejected and honestly had not given a single shit about that game because afterward he couldn't go to Her.

The sun hit his sweaty forehead, making him squint. He grunted when a female-feeling object launched itself into his un-ready arms. Frowning down at her, he rallied his inner asshole, hoping she would leave him the hell alone. She just beamed up at him as if he'd given her a dozen roses and an engagement ring.

Dear god, help me get out of this. Please.

He let her drag him to his car, a brand new Mercedes that he despised, but would live in if it meant escaping from Kelli-with-an-i.

He missed his bike, the one he'd left behind with his life in Nashville, like an amputated limb. The memory sensation of his Mistress' arms around his torso as they took long rides out into the Tennessee countryside still had the power to leave him breathless. However, his training as a proper Southern young man would not be over ridden. He opened Kelli's door, handed her in, and clenched the key fob so tightly that when he opened his hand, a distinctive medallion logo was imprinted on his palm.

Chapter Seven

The odors of Sophie's hot yoga studio centered her. The odd combination of lavender, lemon, and sweat was a familiar comfort. She'd discovered the practice not long after getting released from the hospital, in conjunction with the physical therapy required to inch her way toward recovery. Her favorite part was lying in the hot, humid semi-dark a few minutes before the lights would blaze to life, and the sixty or so barely dressed bodies would rise to their feet to begin the ninety-minute session of stretch and sweat.

Sophie liked to use those fifteen minutes before each session to settle, to get focused and used to the heat in the room, or even to grab a short nap. She hadn't slept well for the last couple of years, despite the daily physical and mental pushing herself to total exhaustion. These aromatic few moments were among the few when she could fully relax.

The yoga kept her fit and her mind sane, as she liked to tell anyone who asked why in the hell she would do such a thing, considering her past injuries. Anyone who hadn't done it, or had tried and given it up, would never understand the perfect balance she found for a couple of hours each day in the zone of a one-hundred-plus degree, fifty percent humidity room.

The lights flickered to life right on cue, and the shushing sound of Lycra and flesh against towel-covered mats began. The practice never changed. The class leader said the same words and the twenty-six postures never altered. She'd needed its consistency in her life at one time, and after six months of forcing herself to show up for it every single day, it almost caused her physical pain when she skipped it. She rolled her shoulders, did her little pre-yoga mental pep talk routine, ignoring everyone around her.

She found it easy to sink into a blank mental space, dare she call it a subspace, when doing the daily torture. Knowing what she did about subspace, she acknowledged this would be as close as she ever went down that particular sensory rabbit hole. She shook her head as the class leader began her script. The same words every time, soothing in their sameness.

By the time they finished the first four postures including wrapping her legs and arms around each other like pretzels and holding some of the most awkward poses the human body might endure—also known as "the warm up," — anxiety still zinged through her. After a year of daily practice, many times she could zone out, and glance up at the final breathing exercise, shocked that the hour and a half had passed already.

Today was not going to be one of those days.

With a heavy sigh, she took a sip of water before heading into the balancing series. Without warning, a strange sensation slithered down her spine. The new and annoying, constantly rattled state she seemed to operate in lately had to stop. She got a grip on her psyche, gave it a shake, used her inner Domme voice, and stared straight ahead into the mirror.

Wedged as she was into one of the more crowded classes, she only had a small sliver of herself visible. She began the set up for standing head-to-knee pose, one of the more difficult ones she'd recently mastered. She kept her standing leg firm, as instructed, with her other straight out in front, her legs a perfect letter L-shape, both hamstrings singing out until adjusting to the stretch.

Her fingers slipped around the ball of her raised foot ever so slightly. Concentration broken, she sucked in a breath and glanced into the mirror, immediately meeting the gaze of the man/boy who'd knocked her world off its axis all those weeks ago.

Goddamned Brody Vaughn was in her god damn yoga class, two god damned rows up.

He was also clutching the bottom of his foot. Sweat poured off him. His face registered simultaneous surprise and dismay at the sight of her.

She lost what remained of her focus and her hands loosened, making her topple forward, and sending the row in front of her murmuring and shifting to make room. Falling out of a posture occurred all the time. Falling flat on the floor like a marionette with its strings cut? Not so much.

She bit her lip, forced away tears of embarrassed frustration, and sat. The instructor never missed a beat, as she made her way toward the hapless practitioner sitting on her ass on her mat and kept up the mantras, the words, the same stupid words every damn day over and over, amen.

"I'm fine." Sophie scrambled to her feet and shot Brody a quick frown of admonition. His already red face flushed a deeper shade, something only someone in tune to the subtle changes of a submissive's signals would notice. He held his damn pose, though, and kept his gaze off hers admirably. Deciding to wait out the pose for the moment, she used the opportunity to observe him.

Every inch of her skin prickled as she took in his black, close-cut hair, broad shoulders, the muscled expanse of his torso, and the most luscious ass she'd seen since, well, since she'd goggled him earlier that day during the team's training session. Her tongue darted out, touching her upper lip of its own accord. She drowned in him, imagining herself touching him, tracing her tongue along all the ink covering his firm flesh.

The man sported more tattoos than she'd ever seen on one body. In addition to the linked chain around his neck, he had elaborate designs on both shoulders, and some calligraphy letters traversed the breadth of his upper back. She tried to make sense of them, but they were random.

It hardly mattered. She'd only seen part of his god-like physique during practices. Now, wearing nothing more than shorts and a sheen of sweat, he was like a living sculpture, his every muscle standing out in bas-relief, begging for her touch.

The bodies in the room shifted, moving on to the next posture, leaving her behind. She jumped, mortified at how naturally her thoughts about the sexy young man skidded right off the rails into visions of ropes, cuffs, whips, those full, kissable lips, and what she'd make him do with them.

"Jesus, woman, get a grip," she muttered under her breath and spent the ensuing seventy minutes using every ounce of energy to avoid looking at him.

Once the class wound down, she pondered skipping the usual five or so minutes she spent relaxing like a limp noodle. She lay there, aware of every small sound around her, negotiating internally for the entire time whether to leap up and escape or to let him stumble out first. Finally, cursing her sudden indecisiveness, she rose, rolled up her mat and left the room, ignoring everyone, including him. She managed to yank her sweat pants over her bare legs, jam a hat down onto her wet hair, and had her hand on the door, escape within her grasp.

"Um, Mizz... uh...." His deep voice hit her low and right where it shouldn't.

She grimaced and turned, fixing a glare of aggravation on her face. When their eyes locked, the abject need in the huge, brown depths of his forced her to stumble.

"Sorry." He took a step away from her.

The small foyer of the yoga studio didn't accommodate the mass of sweaty bodies milling around, trying to regain a collective equilibrium, get re-dressed, and get the hell out of there. Someone shoved into her hip, and she lost her footing. But he wouldn't drop his gaze from hers, and she hung onto it like a lifeline while sweaty bodies floated around them. She leaned close, unable to stop. He latched onto her arm. Startled, she stared at the fingers now encircling her elbow.

She opened her mouth to protest, to tell him to take his mitts off her, until she noticed he had kept her from embarrassing herself further by falling to her butt outside the hot room.

"You can let go now," she said, mildly, feeling an odd sort of rightness in her brain. He tightened his hand on her for a split second and then obeyed, turning his gaze to the floor. A bright, clear vision appeared to her at that split second. She forced it away before it could be more than a foggy image of this man on his knees in front of her.

"Can I buy you a coffee or something?"

"Huh?" She stared at him, dumbfounded, remembering at the last minute to snap her mouth shut. "I mean, no. Um, no thanks."

Escape. That had to be her goal. Get as far away from him and his needy perfection as possible.

"Okay," he said, his face devoid of anything, including disappointment. "See ya around." He moved around her smoothly, his hip grazing hers. He yanked the door open and walked out, leaving her flat-footed in the middle of the milling, post-workout crowd.

• • • •

SIMULTANEOUS SENSATIONS of relaxation and excitement thrummed through Brody's brain. He'd never felt so at ease in his skin yet ready to leap out of it. He floored the Merc, relishing its throaty roar across Interstate 94 toward the nameless, soulless suburbia he now called home. He'd been a big fan of yoga since giving it a try in Nashville, when his coach had forced the entire team to practice it to improve their flexibility.

Desperate for something to do to dispel his ever-increasing state of high alert, he'd Googled hot yoga and found a few locations including Birmingham and Ann Arbor. Figuring he'd not checked out the college town to the west, he headed there. And had run smack into the woman he blamed for his current overwrought state.

He downed the rest of the water in his bottle and opened every window in the expensive, obnoxious car. Of course Sophie Harrison would be waiting for him in the Ann Arbor class. She of the intangible, unexplainable something that he craved but didn't understand since meeting her in that stifling office in her boss lady yet sexy suit, glaring at him as if he'd been caught torturing kittens and not simply showing up for his mandated meeting with the legal department.

He caressed the soft leather steering wheel as the cool fall air blew through the car's interior. Moments like this, his body at rest, his brain on autopilot, memories of his Mistress would blindside him. He gulped at them now, his body hardening under the loose-fitting shorts.

"Shit. Shit. Shit. Shit!" he cried out, smacking the wheel and willing her gone. When would she be gone from his consciousness? Never? Someday?

Arriving at what passed for home, he parked under the huge building, his chest tight with stress. His phone buzzed in the seat next to him. He gripped the wheel, trying to wrap his mind around the hard fact that, at that moment he would just as soon keep driving at sixty miles per hour straight into the wall he currently faced as get out, get a shower, and go pick up Kelli. They had a date. He had to take her to a concert, then bring her home and do his duty by her.

"Help," he whispered to no one, meaning it more than he had ever meant anything in his life. The sensation of being utterly unmoored made his head pound.

He hauled himself out of the German-engineered monstrosity, leaving the windows down, not caring if anyone took the fucker and even pondered leaving the keys on it, posting a sign on the window that said, Steal Me. Such were the depths of his not caring.

By the time he entered his not-quite-penthouse unit, he recalled he'd left his phone on the passenger's seat. Totally not like him. He wasn't the type of person to leave windows down, doors unlocked, to have such blatant disregard for accepted behavior. He stared into the mirror over the front hall table, acknowledging that he simply wasn't the man he used to be, and would likely never be.

Sophie's face wavered across his consciousness. He relived that split second he'd grabbed her arm, asked her out for coffee, and she'd rejected him outside the yoga room.

"Jeez, it was just a cup of coffee," he said under his breath, wandering into the kitchen then downing another full glass of water.

His laptop sat open on the granite-topped island. He tugged it close and hit the touchpad. He'd done some research, if the pages open from three in the morning were any indication. He recalled the itchy, skin-crawling horror of need that drove him to dig deep and find what he required.

And in black and white—okay, red and purple—he'd found it. Madame Katrina, it stated in classic block letters on a sort of velvety looking backdrop. The only image, a tall, leather, high-heeled boot, the sort that he used to lick his way up on command, dominated the center of the screen. The trailing ends of a whip peeked out from around the toe of it, as soft and inviting-looking as he remembered.

With a grimace, he clicked on the scheduling tab and noted the price without flinching. It's amazing what a seven-figure salary will do for a single guy, he thought as he studied the professional calendar-style system. Madame Katrina, Dominatrix for hire. This is what he'd been reduced to.

The investigating he'd done, contacting some former clients who'd agreed to it, all pointed to one conclusion: if he needed a hard discipline session, then Madame K should be his next stop. Do not pass go, do not collect two hundred dollars. Sophie's face flickered to life in his upper brain as the lizard version did something else to him entirely.

Memory of her shock at seeing him in class, the way she'd blatantly checked him out, thinking he didn't know she was doing it, combined with her firm, taut body, mostly bare in hot yoga garb, hardened him all over. Yeah, a trip to see this Madame Katrina should be on his calendar if he was going to be worth a shit to the team that paid his salary. Not to mention keep him from driving his stupid car off the nearest bridge.

His doorbell rang, startling him. He got up, pulling a T-shirt down over his bare torso then rested his forehead agaist the door for a moment. "Hang on a sec," he said before striding back over to his computer to set his date with the mysterious five hundred dollar an hour Dominatrix.

The team had games the next day, Friday, and following Wednesday, and then a long break until a stretch of travel along the West Coast. Maybe, just maybe, he'd get something resembling the old Brody back under the supposed expert hands and whips and ropes of the good Madame. Her address wasn't far from the Black Jacks stadium. Convenient, he mused, without a trace of irony.

Opening the door, he suffered the attentions of Kelli-with-an-i until he woke, naked, wrapped around her nude form, remembering absolutely nothing.

Chapter Eight

Sophie glanced at the private phone buried in her purse, noting a new voice mail. The system she had set up to screen all applicants by requiring them to provide a real name and driver's license number that her assistant ran through several background checks—or they could take their needy egos elsewhere—had served her well so far. Considering her history, she sometimes wondered how she trusted anyone. But through hard experience, she'd found men who desired her special services and were desperate enough to tell her anything she asked. The clients remained anonymous to her after they were screened. She never knew real names or histories.

Only the hulking man who took thirty percent of her fee got the real stories behind the men standing at her door on any given night. By providing screening and bodyguard services during the sessions, Dante Franklin had proven to be her savior, in more ways than one. After she'd done her due diligence, checking out his background.

His latest message informed her she had a new appointment in a couple of weeks. A new client who'd cleared all security hurdles.

"He says to call him Robert," the message concluded. "An experienced sub, he claims. Should be a piece of cake for you, sweetheart."

She smiled at the sound of his deep voice in her ear. A gay man in a long-term, committed relationship, Dante had roamed around the hard-core BDSM scene for a while, been in the military police for ten years, and now served as her right-hand man.

She pondered the reality of a new client, someone who claimed experience at being a submissive for a few moments before turning to the legal tasks surrounding the soccer team. Her two computer monitors displayed several windows, including the latest gossip site that had latched onto the Bad Boys of Detroit like a leech, following them around everywhere they went, finding all the bad, and very little good, best she could tell. The strange thing was that the site had been set up by their own marketing department as a front to bolster buzz about their team members.

Yeah. Talk about a clusterfuck of epic proportions. She hated the thing for a lot of reasons. It made her job a hundred times harder when evidence of misbehavior amongst the players and, in one case, an assistant coach who'd been quickly fired, got smeared all over the Internet within moments of said occurrence. She took notes on the day's collection of gossip on the annoying site, grateful it was nothing serious.

After she'd pointed out that their own organization spreading potentially damaging information and photos about their players should be a painfully obvious stupid decision, the powers that be rallied. Jack led the charge, demanding the whole thing get dropped like the hottest of hot potatoes. Of course, some trolling Internet smart-ass snagged it, slightly altered the name, and it lived on as paparazzi, both amateur and professional, figured out how to earn their own measure of notoriety by posting phone videos and pictures straight to it.

She narrowed her eyes as the screen refreshed itself and a slew of new pictures emerged. At least one good thing had started happening with it—since there were ten total teams in the expansion league the fans who posted on it had a few other targets not just the Black Jacks, although the boys from Detroit were absolutely the darlings of the cheering, and jeering, public.

Thanks to the original marketing ploy, she'd already slogged more hours than necessary, trying to get the team full of overgrown boys out of jams they had no business getting into. It wasn't that professional athletes didn't ever get into trouble, but never before had a group of them gotten into so much, seemingly on camera. Jesus, they might as well call it Black Jack Gentlemen: The Reality Show.

Something on the newly updated site caught her attention. She slid her glasses up her nose. Her close encounter with Brody at the yoga studio had faded, although she'd had to take a series of cold showers to dispel not only the physical but the emotional needy vibe he had slung at her.

She considered herself nothing more than a total stan for him. A one-woman Brody Vaughn stalker fan club. She used the convenient excuse of her position to monitor both his social media accounts. All of which he maintained religiously, and on the level, posting exactly twice a day as instructed by the genius marketing office and making generic comments about training, games, and other soccer matches he watched. Nothing but the basics and only one photo that he'd kept the same for months, as opposed to the Internet promotion whores on the team who seemed to post shirtless photos of themselves ad nauseum.

The addition of a new platform, something called ChitChat which was blowing up in popularity, had given them all a bit of pause since it originated in China. But it seemed not to matter, and they'd all adopted it from the equipment managers to the players to the front marketing office. She hated all of it. It was all nothing more than an excuse to grab personal data plus enough photos of you to create near perfect face recognition. And of course, there were the groupies who used it to keep up a constant video stream of themselves looking perfect while dishing on various members of the team which had caused plenty of drama.

Brody had yet to jump on the ChitChat bandwagon, thank god. He preferred posting photos. One had mesmerized her for nearly an hour when she'd seen it the first time. It was of him leaning on the handlebars of a large motorcycle, one eyebrow slightly cocked, his disheveled, windblown, much longer hair suggesting that he'd just ended a ride. His wide, genuine smile lit up every corner of her brain as if he had flung open the blinds on a bright summer day. His face, shoulders, and arms filled the frame. The longer she studied the lines of his bone structure, put together in such a way to suggest a strong, rugged personality with a hint of darkness, the more obsessed she became. He was a brutally attractive almost-man who had worked hard for his sport, and one she itched to touch, to soothe, to cradle to her in ways she couldn't comprehend.

Sighing, she opened up one of his pages and was surprised to find a new photo tagged by someone named Kelli Carlson. It was Brody, standing next to some skinny chick with too-bright teeth. Sophie's scalp prickled with mounting jealousy as she hit the photo with her cursor, making it surge ten times larger on the screen.

Wearing a dark suit and a tense expression, he had an arm draped around the woman clinging to him. They were positioned on a red carpet of some sort, and Sophie recalled the fundraiser most of the team had attended recently.

She narrowed her eyes, studying the couple on the screen, and suddenly realized who Kelli was. Grant Carlson was a zillionaire inventor of an electric car technology, who'd sold the patent a few years ago and was settled in as Detroit's benevolent benefactor. Her own former law firm, Harrison & Winter, had brokered the patent sale.

It appeared that man's daughter had her claws sunk deep into the soccer player at her side. A man who seemed at once in the moment while wishing he were far, far away. Sophie jumped to her feet and started pacing, unwilling to admit that the fury pinging around in her head made any sense whatsoever. She hated herself then, acting like some kind of stupid, dreamy pre-teen, obsessing over a movie star or a fictional book boyfriend. She berated herself for coveting another woman's man. And for thinking unkind things about the obviously starving young woman.

She leaned on the ledge at the bank of windows, taking in the Black Jack's afternoon training, her eyes going immediately to the goal. Brody had his head thrown back, laughing, revealing that intriguing, inky black chain.

He blocked kicked balls, then used his powerful left leg to send them flying to the far end of the pitch before the team squared off in their usual end-of-practice scrimmage. These were brutal affairs, during which many intra-squad grudges were revealed and excised.

Nicco Garza was making a determined, running beeline for a tall, dark-skinned man she didn't recognize at first. Nicco had been a classic problem child for a while but seemed to have settled, thanks to Parker Rollings, the team's young captain with whom he had struck up a serious relationship.

She'd done her fair share of deflecting requests that Nicco and Parker be used as poster boys for the cause of gay professional athletes. Not that she didn't support what they were doing. She did, but it was their business, not the public's. It seemed to her as though the team ought to focus on their third season of play instead of the high drama of accepting any of the hundreds of requests the marketing office fielded on the couple's behalf. Thank goodness Jack had allowed her to make the final call.

But now, Nicco seemed bent on taking out the player who'd been causing a low-lying rumble of gossip and bad-mouthing about the two men and the fact they had gone so far as to appear in public as a couple.

Pro athletes in general were not terribly supportive of homosexual teammates, although backlash had died down some in the last few years. The tall defender with the stupid, homophobic mouth backed up slowly toward his goal in the face of Nicco's all-out onslaught. He had about half a foot of height on the older Spaniard. But Nicco had zero fear and the second he barreled into the guy, left shoulder down and planted into the other man's chest, his left foot making a pseudo play for the ball at his feet, she grasped just how badly this whole thing could go.

The sheer force of the two strong bodies connecting drove them nearly four feet backwards. The rest of the team froze as the incident played out. Parker, Nicco's boyfriend, one of the few mature men on the team, had already started for them, breaking from his position as forward on the opposing side.

The coaches had taken a step from the sidelines where they usually stood and let the team work out their differences for a few minutes before calling a halt to the chaos. The very bad feeling about the scene unfolding below her began to blossom into anxiety. She pushed away from the window, thinking she should just do her own job and not worry about the field full of raging testosterone and egos. But she couldn't look away.

Brody maintained his position directly in the line of fire when Nicco and his nemesis—Cody, she remembered now—barreled straight for him. He had his hands on his hips, just watching them, not moving. She clutched her neck, willing him to get the hell out of the way. He glanced up for a split second, seeming to look directly at her from all that distance.

"Get out of the way, you stubborn idiot," she whispered into the empty office.

When the inevitable collision with the tall object of her obsession came, she yelped with dismay. The combined pounds and anger of the two men, now entangled, with fists flying, hit him hard, shoving him backward. Brody smacked into the far left post of the goal and went down like a ton of bricks. Metin and Parker fell on the fighters, dragging them apart. It took all four men a few seconds to notice Brody had not gotten up.

Sophie had already dashed out her door toward the elevator by then, knowing she had no business doing it but unable to stop.

Chapter Nine

• • • •

BRODY STARED UP AT the sky.

Since when had the bright blue fall morning clouded over?

He sat up. Or rather, tried to. But his head had been gripped in a vise apparently, and something large was crushing his chest. At first he allowed the dreamy, floating sensation to take him, wishing he were restrained the way he wanted to be, with ropes and shackles, tied down and at his Mistress' mercy.

Strange noises wove in and out of the whooshing that had taken up residence between his ears. The ocean noise equally soothed and annoyed. He got the distinct sensation of being on a pitching, yawing boat. And with it, came a horrific nausea twisting his gut. He shook his head. Or he tried to. When the mild panic that lit his consciousness bloomed in his chest, he heard her voice.

"Get out of my way, damn you. Move!" Her. Sophie. She'd shown up, here, wherever the fuck *here* might be. She'd help him figure this out.

As quickly as he opened his eyes, he closed them to stave off a sudden freight train of intense pain barreling through his skull. The world faded, flickered out, plunging him into darkness, terror, and the alone space he once sought but now avoided.

He fought it, muscling his way up to consciousness, surrounded by a bizarre array of faces hovering over him. Goddamn, but his head hurt.

"Stay still," his coach demanded, moving to make room for some guys in uniforms. *Why were the cops here?* He blinked, and that simple act sent another indescribable shaft of pain from his skull all the way down his spine. "Hang on, Vaughn. Don't move."

He tried to disobey, but he'd been rendered immobile, live rats of panic scratching at his rib cage.

A sound escaped his lips. "I...can't."

"Fuck," Metin barked out, rising to let the paramedics lift him onto a board and up to a gurney.

Brody blinked once more which seemed to be the only movement left to him.

"Step aside." Her voice broke through his panic again. "Goddamn it, let me see him." He tried to turn his head. She appeared over him, her deep blue eyes full of concern, her thick hair tumbling out of its tie-back framing her face. She touched his cheek. "Why didn't you get out of their way?" she asked, her face set in worried lines.

He swallowed. Tried to shift his position, happily surprised to find his body cooperated. Just before a giant, horrific pain enveloped him.

"Ow," he whispered, as the monster devoured him from the neck down. He shivered and his teeth rattled in his jaw when the medics rolled him out into the sunlight. His chest ached and his head pounded. Blessed, pain-free darkness descended in seconds.

• • • •

HE WOKE, DISORIENTED and terrified to try to move his arms and legs. Remembering every single moment of the collision, he recalled it had not even been that big a deal. He'd absorbed the force of the two men barreling into him and stepped back of his own accord, but someone's elbow connected with his sternum, and a different one with his chin, making him stumble. Apparently, he must have clonked the back of his skull on the left goal post hard enough to end up in the hospital.

He grimaced, forced his arm to move, lifting one then the other over his head, their familiar, inked surfaces reassuring. Bending one knee and the other, he rolled his ankles around and finally tried to sit, the movement causing a rush of nausea so fierce he fell back onto the pillow.

A nurse rushed in, fussing around him while the room did funny tricks, spinning and warping. A concussion, after all his years of play, thanks to those fucking assholes who'd been gunning for each other during a scrimmage. *Jesus*. He groaned again, trying not to puke. The nurse put a small plastic bowl in front of his mouth and he obligingly filled it.

"Gah." He wiped his lips and accepted the Styrofoam cup of ice water. But he shook so much he could barely drink. He finally gave up and flopped back on the pillow, dropping into an immediate, dreamless sleep.

• • • •

A DEEP RUMBLE THAT had to be the club manager, Rafe, and the heavily accented sound of his coach, Metin woke him the second time. Then a female lilt hit his ears. Relief coursed through him at the sound as he fought his way to the surface, shoving aside the bizarre curtains of unconsciousness.

Four people stood at the end of his bed, the manager and coach as he suspected, and a tall guy in a suit—Jack Gordon, one of the team owners.

However, the female voice didn't belong to the woman he wanted to see at his bedside, but to a tall, angular, lady doctor with a firm set to her jaw. "This man is not to play a minute of soccer until he has been fully evaluated, we run an MRI since the CT scan isn't showing anything, *and* he passes the head injury team's evaluation."

Jack spoke, stepping in front of the other two with a natural authority. "How long will all that take?"

She consulted her tablet computer, tapped on it a few seconds, leaving the men and Brody to stew and worry. "At least three weeks, but my preference, considering his symptoms, is two months."

They all groaned. Brody struggled to sit, steadfastly ignoring the way the room did an alarming fuzz-out on him. "I'm fine." His low, froggy voice alarmed him. He cleared it and repeated the words.

The doctor glared at the men in front of her. "This is my patient, gentlemen, and unless he signs out against medical advice, I'm afraid you'll have to take concerns about your soccer team elsewhere." She put a hand on Brody's blanketed foot. Just as he acknowledged relief that he could feel it, the room became a truly bizarre shade of purple before disappearing altogether. The last thing he heard before the darkness filled him was his coach.

"Oh, shit," his coach said. "He's out again."

"If you don't kill those two fucking assholes who did this, I will," Brody said, but it came out sounding like drunk pig Latin.

• • • •

SOMETHING COOL AND soft touched his face. He rolled onto his side and tried to pull it close, to cradle it to his body. A distinctly female smell invaded his nose. Sharp perfume, and soap and all the things he associated with.... He forced his eyes open to find Kelli, her huge, fake tits looming out of a low-cut sweater right over him. He groaned and rolled the other way unwilling to face that particular nightmare.

Where was she? After rushing down to the field from her office, Sophie had disappeared. *Why hasn't she come?* He didn't want Kelli here. He ignored her until he heard the clickety-clack of her retreating high heels.

He got up, determined not to lie there like an invalid another minute. Clutching the portable IV pole, he found the bathroom, emptied his bladder for what seemed like an hour, nearly falling to the floor at the damn toilet. Glancing at the clock over his bed, he saw the numbers but didn't register the meaning of them. *What day is it? How long have I been flopping around in a head-injured stupor?*

A low, threatening noise came from his stomach and intense hunger washed over him. Making his tethered way back into the room, he hit the nurse button and asked for food. He waited in the reclining chair near the bed to eat it, unwilling to get back in that bed lest he stay there forever. Just as the surprisingly decent, if somewhat bland meal disappeared off the plates and into his empty gut, the door creaked open.

"Hi," Sophie said. "Brody? You in here?"

He cleared his throat, his body tingling in a familiar way, and he had a second of sheer relief that he had not maintained the scary temporary paralysis he'd experienced right after the collision. Wiping his face and trying not to be worried that he smelled like the inside of a soccer bag, he pushed the tray aside.

"Don't get up," she insisted, emerging into the light thrown by the television. "I just need to...ah...discuss something with you. To make sure you aren't going to...."

His ears rang but not from the injury. "I'm not suing anybody if that's why you're here." Disappointment rang through him. She was only doing her job.

"Oh, well, okay. I won't make you sign anything. Give me a little credit." Her smile lit the dark corners of his brain. She'd used it as an excuse to come to see him. But all that mattered was her presence in his room.

Exhaustion overtook him. His whole body shook not because of his condition but her proximity. His eyes played tricks on him, making her loom large. She touched his face, moving to his shoulders, rubbing out tension. His face burned, but he took a breath, determined to enjoy the moment with her flesh on his as perfect as he had anticipated it would be.

Her face appeared near his, her lips so...close, so full and perfect. His pulse raced and then calmed. She touched his cheek once more.

"It will be all right," she whispered near his ear. Her fingertips brushed something from his face. These were the last things he remembered before dropping into the familiar, annoying, deep sleep of the recently concussed.

Chapter Nine

Brody stared up at the sky, wondering. Since when had the bright blue fall morning clouded over?

He sat up. Or rather, tried to. But his head was gripped in a vise, and something large was crushing his chest. At first he allowed the dreamy, floating sensation to take him, wishing he were restrained the way he wanted to be, with ropes and shackles, tied down and at his Mistress' mercy.

Strange noises wove in and out of the whooshing that had taken up residence between his ears. The ocean noise equally soothed and annoyed. He got the distinct sensation of being on a pitching, yawing boat. He shook his head. Or he tried to. When the mild panic that lit his consciousness bloomed in his chest, he heard her voice.

"Get out of my way, damn you. Move!" Sophie. She was here, wherever the fuck here might be. She'd help him figure this out.

As quickly as he opened his eyes, he closed them to stave off a freight train of intense pain barreling through his skull. The world faded, flickered out, plunging him into darkness, terror, and the alone space he once sought. He fought it, muscling his way up to consciousness, surrounded by a bizarre array of faces hovering over him.

"Stay still," his coach demanded, moving to make room for some guys in uniforms. Why were the police here? Was he in trouble? He blinked, and that simple act sent another indescribable shaft of pain from his skull all the way down his spine. "Hang on, Vaughn. Don't move."

He tried to disobey, but he'd been rendered immobile. Panic scrabbled around inside his rib cage.

A sound escaped his lips. "I can't."

"Fuck," Metin barked out, rising to let the paramedics lift him onto a board and up to a gurney. "Fucking fuck."

Brody blinked once more which seemed to be the only movement left to him.

"Step aside." Her voice broke through his panic again. "Let me see him." She appeared over him, her deep blue eyes full of concern, her thick hair tumbling out of its tie-back framing her face. She touched his cheek. "Why didn't you get out of their way?" she asked, her face set in worried lines.

He swallowed. Tried to shift his position, happily surprised to find his body cooperated. Just before a giant, horrific pain enveloped him.

"Ow," he whispered, as an agony monster devoured him from the neck down. He shivered and his teeth rattled when the medics rolled him out into the sunlight. His chest ached and his head pounded. Blessed, pain-free darkness descended in seconds.

• • • •

HE WOKE, DISORIENTED and too terrified to try to move his arms and legs. Recalling every single moment of the collision, he realized that it hadn't even been that hard of a hit. He'd absorbed the force of the two men barreling into him and stepped back of his own accord, but someone's elbow connected with his sternum, and a different one with his chin, making him stumble. Then he must have clonked the back of his skull on the left goal post hard enough to end up in the hospital.

He grimaced, forced his arm to move, lifting one then the other over his head, their familiar, inked surfaces reassuring. Bending one knee and the other, he rolled his ankles around and finally tried to sit, the movement causing a rush of nausea so fierce he fell back onto the pillow with a loud groan.

A nurse rushed in, fussing around him while the room did funny tricks, spinning and warping. A concussion, after all his years of play, thanks to those fucking assholes who'd been gunning for each other during a scrimmage. Jesus. He groaned again, trying not to puke. The nurse put a small plastic bowl in front of his mouth and he obligingly filled it.

"Gah." He wiped his lips and accepted the Styrofoam cup of ice water. But he shook so much he could barely drink. He finally gave up and flopped back on the pillow, dropping into an immediate, dreamless sleep.

• • • •

A DEEP RUMBLE THAT had to be the club manager's, answered by the heavily accented voice of his coach woke him the second time. Then a female lilt hit his ears. Relief coursed through him as he fought his way to the surface, shoving aside the bizarre curtains of unconsciousness.

Four people stood at the end of his bed, the manager and coach as he suspected, and a tall guy in a suit he recognized as Jack Gordon, one of the team's owners.

However, the female voice didn't belong to the woman he wanted to see at his bedside, but to a lady doctor with a firm set to her jaw. "This man is not to play a minute of soccer until he has been fully evaluated, we run an MRI since the CT scan isn't showing anything, and he passes the head injury team's evaluation."

Jack spoke, stepping in front of the other two with a natural authority. "How long will all that take?"

She consulted her tablet, tapping around on it a few seconds, leaving the men and Brody to stew. "At least three weeks, but my preference, considering his symptoms, is two months."

They all groaned. Brody struggled to sit, steadfastly ignoring the way the room did an alarming fuzz-out on him. "I'm fine." His low, froggy voice sounded strange. He cleared it and repeated the words.

The doctor glared at the men in front of her. "This is my patient, gentlemen, and unless he signs out against medical advice, I'm afraid you'll have to take concerns about your soccer team elsewhere." She put a hand on Brody's blanketed foot. Just as he acknowledged relief that he could feel it, the room morphed into a bizarre shade of purple before disappearing altogether. The last thing he heard before the darkness fell once more him was his coach.

"Oh, shit," his coach said. "He's out again."

"If you don't kill those two fucking assholes who did this, I will," Brody said, but it came out sounding like drunk pig Latin.

Something cool and soft touched his face. He rolled onto his side and tried to pull it close, to cradle it to his body. A sharp feminine cologne smell invaded his nose. He forced his eyes open to find Kelli, her huge, fake tits looming out of a low-cut sweater right over him. He groaned and rolled the other way unwilling to face that particular nightmare.

Where was Sophie? After rushing down to the field from her office, she'd disappeared. Why hasn't she come? He didn't want Kelli here. He ignored her until he heard the clickety-clack of her retreating high heels.

He sat up on the side of the bed, determined not to lie there like an invalid another minute. Clutching the portable IV pole, he found the bathroom, emptied his bladder for what seemed like an hour, nearly falling to the floor when he was done. Glancing at the clock over his bed, he saw the numbers but didn't register the meaning of them. What day is it? How long have I been flopping around in a head-injured stupor?

A low, threatening noise came from his stomach as intense hunger washed over him. Making his tethered way back into the room, he hit the nurse button and asked for food. He waited in the reclining chair near the bed to eat it, unwilling to get back in that bed lest he stay there forever. Just as the surprisingly decent, if somewhat bland, meal disappeared off the plates and into his empty gut, the door creaked open.

"Brody? You in here?" Sophie said from the doorway.

He cleared his throat, his body tingling in a familiar way. Wiping his face and trying not to be worried that he smelled like the inside of a soccer bag, he pushed the tray aside.

"Don't get up," she insisted, emerging into the light thrown by the television. "I just need to discuss something with you. To make sure you aren't going to...."

His ears rang, but not from the injury. "I'm not suing anybody, if that's why you're here." Disappointment clanged in his ears. She was only here to do her job.

"Okay." Her smile lit the dark corners of his brain when he realized that she'd used that as an excuse to come to see him. But all that mattered was her presence.

Exhaustion overtook him. His whole body began to tremble. His eyes played tricks on him, making her loom large. She touched his face, then his shoulder. His face burned, but he took a breath, determined to enjoy the moment with her flesh against his. A sensation as perfect as he had anticipated.

Her face appeared near his, her lips were so close, so full and perfect. His pulse raced and then calmed. She touched his cheek once more.

"It will be all right," she whispered near his ear. Her fingertips brushed something from his face. These were the last things he remembered before dropping into the familiar, annoying, deep sleep of the recently concussed.

Chapter Ten

Two weeks later, Brody took up a spot on the sidelines, helping Metin train the two back-up goalies for the duration. He was forbidden from any direct contact or play under dire threats from the head injury team at the hospital. Sophie had memorized every word of the doctors' orders.

The moment he'd nearly broken down in the hospital room stayed with her, and she replayed it over and over, thumbing through it, seeking ways she might have handled it differently, but always came to the same conclusion; the man had no one in his corner. When faced with it as he had been in the hospital, he exuded a sort of agonizing unhappiness that made her want to gather him up and spirit him away into her home, her life, and yes, her bed.

She had his background committed to memory. The mother dead of an overdose, the dramatic rescue from the rattletrap home and subsequent placement in foster care. There were four foster placements but never anything permanent.

His stellar career as a player in high school, state cups, regional and national championships, led to a too-early recruitment from a major league soccer team that he'd turned down in favor of a full-ride scholarship to Vanderbilt. His senior year, the Commodores men's soccer team won the NCAA national championship, beating a highly favored Indiana team.

Young Brody stayed off gossip radars in school. The only strange thing that stood out about him was that he never received his degree. He'd left the school with a three-point-five GPA in business. But he never graduated, thanks to an incomplete in a marketing class during his senior year. Pondering his personnel file in her typical stalker-ish way, she wondered what happened to make him no longer care that he reaped the rewards of what she assumed would be a very tough education at a premier private university. Something told her it had everything to do with that tattooed chain around his neck.

He'd come to the Black Jacks after several years bouncing around major league soccer, getting minimal playing time. But every time he took the field he proved himself as one of the coolest heads in the goal, which was the reason why Rafe had wanted him and why they'd paid a fortune to buy out his previous contract.

She leaned back in her chair and stretched, wishing she had time for a quick nap since she'd gotten up early and had a new client to meet that night. After focusing on her job for a few more hours, she packed up her laptop and headed home with a wave as she walked by the marketing department. On the days when she had to transform, to earn the money she charged for her services, she required time, space, and solitude to get where she needed to be in her head.

She always went straight to the downtown loft when she had her night job, skipping the fake normal of her house in Ann Arbor. Thoughts of her lawyer's last email to her buoyed her. The fact that she'd scraped and clawed her way clear of the personal bankruptcy she'd had to declare after the accident made her smile as she made her way into the loft. The past several years had been harrowing, but it appeared she would emerge with some of her sanity and future intact. She showered in the large bathroom, ever grateful for her partner's calm presence. He'd opened the place up then left her alone, saying he'd be back and outside the door as usual by ten o'clock, the time set to meet Robert.

He always packed the fridge full of her favorite foods—berries, granola, and fresh squeezed orange juice. She ate and drank, stared at the news on her phone without absorbing it, then walked over to open the small, two-person hot tub toward the back of the loft.

When she first dreamed this project up, she'd been talking with Dante at a lame lifestyle party she'd gotten dragged to. Her body was still stiff and sore from the accident and surgeries, her bank account was empty, her heart aching. It's how she discovered her current business partner, the giant man who now regarded her as his savvy, leather-wearing, whip-toting younger sister.

She'd been bought out of her law partnership, but her share had been worth just enough to keep her off food stamps after absorbing a record-breaking hospital bill and finding out her name had been used to run up three credit cards over the course of the same year. Thanks to the man she'd met, fallen for, and hoped was The One.

He was one all right. One huge asshole. She refused to acknowledge his name, even in her mind. When his motorcycle skidded off the road between Ann Arbor and Dexter and left her within shouting distance of death from internal injuries and burns, he'd disappeared like the thief he was. She'd been lucky some bicyclers had been out for an early spring jaunt or she'd certainly not be sitting in this hot tub getting into her mental space, ready to bind, whip, tease, and whatever else her client demanded in order for him to get off, get right, or get real.

Sophie tried not to picture the man who'd ruined her and tried to kill her, now that she would acknowledge what that last bike ride was meant to accomplish. They had exchanged personal vows. She wore his collar, and he supposedly had a great job—all a part of his long con.

After a couple of years together, she'd been utterly, completely duped. While he'd been unable to cash in on her million-dollar life insurance policy, it wasn't for lack of trying. When he disappeared, she hadn't pursued him. Focusing instead on her recovery, both physical and financial, figuring he surely wouldn't be stupid enough to emerge in her life ever again. Besides, the few times she tried to explain their relationship to people who might help her, she got nothing but shocked looks and a lot of, "well, you let him tie you up and whip you so maybe you shouldn't have done that." So she stopped trying.

An angry scar glared at her. She considered it her beacon of stupidity. It ran around her abdomen to her back. She touched it, acknowledging that simple plastic surgery might rid her of it. But she kept it to remind her of the mistake she'd made with a man she trusted with everything, including her life.

She'd lost her spleen, one kidney, and sustained a compound fracture that almost cost her a leg, and that still ached in the cold. But the lasting token of her ill-considered years spent as a submissive were buried deep in her psyche, invisible on the surface. It had turned her into an insomniac, exercise-obsessed and emotionally detached from everything. Along with the dark physical scar she would touch, on occasion, as a reminder of why Madame Katrina existed at all.

"Hey, you all right in here, sunshine?" Dante wandered in, holding a mug of something that smelled delicious. Her buried caffeine freak twitched somewhere in her memory. Those days were long gone, along with the über-bitchy, know-it-all persona she'd used to shove away the one man who'd been perfect and driven her straight into the arms of one who was the polar opposite of perfect.

"Hey," she said, wrapping a towel around her body. She stood in front of her closet of Domme-wear and pondered the options. Many new clients stated their preferences for her garb and attitude on the form her website provided. Robert merely said, "surprise me." She bit the side of her nail. At a loss, and aggravated about it.

Going with the hard bitch thing tonight, she decided as she pulled on leather pants and stiletto boots, topped with a black bra and nothing more. Dropping everything but thoughts of Robert and his unknown needs from her mind, she strode out to the main room, noting Lance had lit all the candles, turned on the gas fireplace, and had the state-of-the-art sound system cranked to, of all things, a Bob Marley song.

She sighed, annoyed, but glad of his presence all the same. He was draped across the large leather chair nearest the fireplace, cradling the ubiquitous coffee to his chest and bellowing out the lyrics along with the stereo.

"Not the sort of mood music I typically go for." She stretched out her quads and hamstrings. Something felt off in her head, and she hated that, because it didn't bode well for her client. Madame Katrina was nothing if not totally customer-service focused. No one left her dungeon dissatisfied. Not if she could help it.

Dante grinned as the song wound down. Then he said "Alexa! Play Madam's Warm Up Playlist." Hardcore grunge started to pound through the cavernous space.

She smiled. "Much better. Thanks. Is it show time?"

He glanced at his watch, then rose and put on his suit coat. She wondered, not for the first time, where he got his clothes. It would take something like a hundred yards of expensive wool to make just one of those suits. He was positively edible, even dressed in sweat pants and a T-shirt. But when he was dressed to work for her it took him to a whole new level. She whistled at him.

"Stop ogling me, bitch," he said, his eyes shining.

"I can window shop, can't I?" She cocked her hip and batted her lashes at him. "Just 'cause I can't buy the goods?"

"Yeah," he said in his low, movie-star worthy voice. He straightened his tie. Never in her life had she met a man more comfortable in his own skin. Amazing, considering all the things he'd done to end up here, a gay male now married to a well-known attorney with political ambitions who served as business partner, bodyguard, and IT consultant to a Bitch-for-Hire. "You can stare. It feeds my ego."

Startled by a knock at the door, they glanced in unison at the clock on the wall. He'd set it to chime within ten minutes of the end time of the sessions.

"Robert is an eager youngster." Dante dimmed the lights and shooed her back so she could make an entrance for full effect.

Sophie blinked. "Youngster?" she managed, but it came out in a high squeak. Sweat popped out on her upper back, and dripped in a familiar, hot yoga-like way down her skin. No. That was ridiculous. She was only projecting.

"Yeah. But he checked out. Never fear, boss lady." He pointed at her and winked. "Ready?"

She gulped and nodded, her mouth dry enough to spit cotton. And looking back, she would never be able to explain how she knew who'd be walking through the door. Dante shot her a funny look.

"Go on," she said, unwilling to say anymore. She was finally going to have the encounter she and Brody Vaughn had set in motion weeks ago.

The urge to cancel the whole thing and save her soul in the process made her dizzy with a sort of lusty anticipation combined with gut-churning panic.

"Open the door." She put a hand on either side of the backlit doorway to the playroom.

A man stepped in. He was dressed in a well-cut suit. The sight of his familiar face prompted the oddest knee-jerk thought from her. He needs a haircut, she mused as she took in the hair he'd let grow since his accident. Then he stepped into the light, smiling, until she moved forward and gave him a full view.

Chapter Eleven

Brody's brain shut down when he spotted her silhouetted in the doorway. Not an unusual reaction, at least in his limited experience. His Mistress, the marketing professor he'd approached about a scheduling problem during a particularly rough patch in his sophomore year, had been his first real experience in bondage, fetish, submission of any kind.

He had meant to keep it that way, to file it all away under Brody Learns a Lesson, never to revisit it. It had been scary and exquisite. A perfect, sexy, learning experience, or so he believed. Brittle memories of punishment, discipline and flat-out kink fests he enjoyed for nearly three years passed through him during the five or so seconds it took for the woman to step into the light.

Stumbling back, he sat down hard when the backs of his legs hit a chair. His palms itched, his brain boiled, and the creeping sensation of, well, of course. Who else? flashed across his consciousness. He did know, had known, or at least had willed it into reality when he made the appointment.

While he may have been short on experience other than what he had learned from his Mistress, he remained acutely in tune to his own needs and to how those around him might meet them. He'd guessed it about her the split second she'd turned to face him, her bored expression blown apart by his presence. Something about the pure light of fate that seemed to burst out of her eyes calmed him, making him more ready for her than ever.

She hesitated, as if sensing his change of attitude from terror to acceptance. Suppressing a shiver and the urge to call out to her, he stayed seated and silent, ready to assume whatever position she demanded of him. And how, he mused, as his cock hardened fast under his zipper.

Oh, god, please let her be fond of canes.

"What the fuck are you doing here?" she asked.

"Are you not Madame Katrina?" The strength of his voice surprised him. His inner submissive was already whimpering, cowed, and eager. She got up in his face, her raw, animal, purely female scent whipping through him, dizzying him as he rose to his feet. Sweat beaded his brow. His lungs squeezed, incapable of proper function.

Her eyes blazed when she shoved him back down to the chair. He stared at the pointy boot heel dug into his thigh and had to grip the chair arms to stop from grabbing it and kissing it.

"Don't talk back to me, Robert." Her harsh voice rang in his ears.

The way she spit out his name made him feel three inches tall. A familiar buzzing noise took up residence in his brain. A welcome whiteness edged his vision. He smiled, still focusing on the shiny leather, groaning when its heel point penetrated the fabric of his trousers.

He stayed still, awaiting her command like the well-trained submissive he'd been. The room hummed with erotic energy, but she stayed silent, letting it spin out and ramp up until he was ready to fly apart at the seams.

She flicked the flogger she must have had hidden behind her back against his torso, more for effect than anything, since his flesh remained covered by the suit. He shifted to release some pressure. The white space descended further. He felt it, tasted it in the back of his throat. Yearned for it in ways he'd been tamping down under layers of self-denial.

Without another word, she spun around and walked away from him. Taking boot heel, whip, and those deep blue eyes he'd been drowning in nightly since meeting her away from him, leaving him bereft. He watched her retreat, licking his lips at the sight of her leather-covered ass. He allowed his gaze to move up the line of her bare back and neck, taking her all in.

He stopped, frowning. "Mistress," he said, again with a voice that surprised him with its strength. "What is that? What happened to you?" He pointed at an angry-looking scar. It wrapped around her waist, its red, puckered edges clear against the white of her skin. It burned his brain. Forced his hands into fists at the thought of her hurt by anyone.

She whirled around, fury clear on her face. "Stand up," she commanded, pointing the flogger at him. "Stand up, Robert, and take everything off. I mean everything." Her voice had gotten hoarse, shaky. He rose. "Slowly. So I can watch you."

Hard wired to obey, he rose and slipped out of shoes and coat, using slow movements, as she had commanded. She stripped out of what little she wore, leaving him fumbling with buttons and breathing too heavy to focus. She'd revealed every glorious inch of her amazing body to his eyes, which shocked him. Usually it took his Mistress a while to join him skin-to-skin, using the first hours or so of their playtime to tease him to peaks of frothy frustration before forcing him back down. Or smacking his ass and thighs so hard with a cane he would drop into his subspace, and remain a dreamy, almost-drowsy lump she used to her content. Riding him like a cowgirl, getting off on his body over and over and over until she allowed him to come up for air.

Those sessions were the scariest. The ones where he lost count of the hours and only existed for her pleasure. Aware, but at the same time, not. Forbidden to enjoy, lest he show weakness via an unapproved orgasm. He experienced a brief moment of regret. What had he done? What had he allowed that woman to do to his sexual psyche?

He shook all over once he completed the undressing, placing each layer of suit coat, socks, trousers, shirt, tie, underwear, all on the chair behind him. Something about the whole scene shifted, seemed to tilt, as if they were on a ship that listed to the port side, about to send them both tumbling head over heels into the abyss.

They stood, facing each other, with nothing but air and bare flesh between them. He smelled her lust, her readiness for him. And suddenly he wanted something more than to be tied up, whipped, caned, wax tortured, or nipple clamped. He wanted to be inside her, to make love to her, hold her close and draw out the most exquisite climax from her lush beauty. He would make it his job to assure her pleasure. She stepped back, as if reading his mind.

Then, with a speed that surprised him, she reached over her head and yanked down a set of metal restraints. "Raise your arms, Robert." She caressed his name while fastening his wrists, letting the tips of her nipples graze his skin. Her mouth trailed down his neck and she licked her way along the chain inked in honor of His Mistress. The woman who had perhaps topped him a little harder than necessary.

A small voice started up with that tune in the back of his head. She had used him, then tossed him out on his ear when she got worried about her precious job.

"Shh...." Sophie whispered, taking her time tracing his tattoos with her tongue and fingertips, setting him on fire until he yanked against the restraints.

He sighed when she licked his abdomen and kept going lower, exploring every nook and possible cranny of him. "Mmmm...." He spread his legs and watched her work, his brain going a thousand miles a minute.

"Robert," she whispered, sliding back up his body, skin-on-skin, before gripping his aching cock. "Would you like to come?" Her palm moved across him, soft, tight, and perfect.

He hissed, his hips jerking at her added pressure. He closed his eyes to think about soccer or something, anything except how badly he wanted to come.

"No," he croaked out. "I can't."

"Oh, I think you can. And you most definitely should." She rubbed her naked body along his, using her exquisite hand to torture. Her teeth found his nipple, his one trigger, the one thing he'd had to fight to control so his Mistress could have her pleasure first. Then Sophie let go, leaving him quivering.

The deep blue of her gaze did something visceral to him. Something that had nothing to do with her flesh on his flesh, with her bare skin against his. And it cleared his head completely. He opened his mouth to say something like "Please release me and let me show you how much pleasure I can bring you." But she kissed him before he could speak, plundering his mouth with hers, her sweet, probing tongue forceful, yet gentle. This was one thing he'd missed during his years of fetish play. His Mistress preferred her distance. She liked to ride him, be fucked by him, but had only allowed him to kiss her once in nearly three years. And that, the very day she kicked him to the curb.

He groaned and let the white space take him. He didn't even recognize the onrushing sensation of orgasm until she broke away from him, her eyes bright. At the release of that most erotic of contacts—the kiss— his nerve endings thrummed and blood flooded his face. The perfection of climax consumed him completely, and he cried out at the near pain of it, having forgotten how it felt when coaxed out of him the way he preferred.

He shook, rattling the bonds on his wrists. Confusion washed through him. She hadn't used anything but her mouth, the simple shackles from the ceiling, and her naked self.

"God," he said, but it came out in barely a whisper. His throat burned and his chest ached. He had come like a teenager, with no thought or attention to her needs. But the orgasm had cleared his head, and he was more sated than he had been in years. How did she do that?

"Ah, alas, no, just me, Madame Katrina."

She stepped back. Her chest heaving with her attempt to control her own ragged breathing. But she turned away, giving him a luscious rear view when she disappeared into a room, then re-emerged wrapped in a black silk short robe. She dropped into a leather chair and observed him. He tugged at the restraints. Their bite didn't have the remembered effect. He didn't like them. He wanted them off so he could scoop the woman in front of him into his arms and never let her go.

"What's wrong, Robert?" she asked, shifting, so the robe fell open, giving him a clear view of the pink of her labia. "Wait. Don't speak," she said, holding up a hand. "I get to come now." He gulped as she touched one of her full breasts, caressed her own nipple, and dropped the other hand between her legs.

"No," he blurted out, surprised but not caring. He would not allow this to happen. "Let me. Please. Let me. I want to... I need...."

She kept rubbing and teasing her pussy, then stopped and put her fingertips to her mouth. "You want to do what, Robert?" She put extra emphasis on his name. "Tell me."

He frowned, a surprising emotion filling his gut. It took him a few seconds to recognize it as anger. Her attitude pissed him off. He didn't want this, didn't want to be in this position anymore. He wanted to be more for her. He yanked at the metal, wincing when his sore wrists hit the cuffs' edges again.

"I want to make love to you, Sophie."

She sat up. The robe fell from her shoulders. The slow burn of desire rolling around in his brain scared him, considering how he'd been programmed to take pleasure from the pain. He liked it, this new sort of urge.

"Release me. Please," he said, his voice low. She rose to her feet, leaving the robe behind. He kept his gaze on hers as she reached up and unlocked the cuffs. Taking a deep breath and getting a full head of her lusty aroma, he let his arms drop until he held her close. She smiled for a half second, giving him a bright, shining shaft of hope.

"You can go now," she said, keeping her tone sexy, as if she were saying something else. It confused him. Her next action didn't. She stepped out of his arms, plucked the robe from the chair, and put it back on. "No charge. But don't come back. I mean it."

Dismayed, sick at heart, and embarrassed, he dressed and left, but not before dropping the full three hour fee on the table by the door. His heartbeat was normal, and his head perfectly clear. He understood what he wanted. And that sudden, crystal-clear realization terrified him more than the thought of never seeing her again.

Chapter Twelve

Sophie lay awake for hours, the usual calm that descended over her body and mind after a nice, hard discipline session for a client remaining elusive.

Well, wonder why, genius? You fucked that up, pure and simple. What in the hell were you thinking?

She groaned, rolled onto her stomach, and dragged the pillow over her head. As if hiding from this disaster she'd set in motion was possible. All because she lost it and let a man into her head, forcing her body to do utterly stupid things and ruining the night for them both.

"Fuck it." She jumped out of bed and tugged a sweatshirt over the T-shirt she normally wore to sleep. The clock displayed the shocking early hour on the bedside table. Why not get an hour's worth of research done before heading into her normal daytime routine?

Never mind, she'd lain awake literally all night, unable to banish the sight of Brody's face when he told her—no, commanded her—to release his wrists. Jesus. She had responded as if he were the Dom. Despite his bound physical position, he'd called the shots. Goddamn him.

After making coffee, she flipped on the TV for background noise to force out the rattling reality of what had happened between them in her lair, in her goddamned Madame Katrina space. The one place where she could be safe. She'd been weak, as always, when faced with a strong male.

A couple of hours spent trolling the gossip sites for her to-do list the next week settled her nerves. A strange clinking noise made her jump in surprise. The laptop glowed unhelpfully. It sang out again, and she noted an icon she rarely used down at the bottom of her screen. It had a red circle on it, and the number 2. She sighed. Probably her boss, a fellow notorious early-riser and list-maker, deciding to use the chat function to get their workday off to a solid start. If he'd been checking out the same sites she'd been, then they did need to discuss a few things.

Deciding to pour a cup of coffee before tackling a Jack Gordon morning bitch session, she settled back into her seat, then clicked the chat icon. But she immediately got distracted by a news flash on the TV screen.

She looked back at her laptop, unwilling to accept the news in front of her. The words, Black Jack Heroes? was tattooed into her brain. She froze when the chat message from Brody Vaughn appeared. At the same time she heard what the talking head on the tv was reporting, and noticed that her phone was buzzing all the way across the kitchen counter. Then she recalled that Jack had gone on a wife-imposed vacation, overseas or some place well out of reach on purpose for a few weeks.

"Harrison," she whispered into the device, still staring, open-mouthed, at the television. "Jesus, Metin, what happened?"

"Can you get down here?"

"Already headed there," she said before hanging up and re-reading Brody's message:

Bad news. Rick and Nate were in an accident at some bar. Can you meet us at Detroit Receiving?

She thumbed through her contacts in her phone, knowing she had every one of the men on the team programmed into it. Frowning, she did a double take back through the list. Why the hell he didn't show up under B? Cursing, she hit V, hoping to find him by his last name.

The damn thing populated from her official team records, thanks to her efficient secretary. Her pulse raced as memories of the man's dark, intense eyes shot across her consciousness in her heightened freak-out state. Robert Vaughn. Surely that wasn't right.

She ran to the bedroom, threw on some dressier clothes, and yanked her hair back. Foregoing makeup, she stuck her feet in heels and grabbed her phone, which opened automatically to the contact: Robert J. Vaughn. She hit send message and typed fast.

On my way.

See you there, he responded.

She drove, processing what she was going to face. Two of the team's players had been at a nightclub, dancing with a few girls, one of whom had just broken up with her boyfriend. Said boyfriend showed up with a gang of friends and a bad attitude. He'd manhandled the girl off the dance floor. Nate, the backup goalie for the team, a young kid with a shock of strawberry blond hair, a male-model perfect body, and an adorable accent that made girls swoon with delight at his every utterance, had pulled a hero move and gotten in a fistfight with the boyfriend.

Witnesses stated one of the boyfriend's buddies pulled out a gun and shot Nate in the leg. Rick, Nate's former teammate in the Irish league, and one of the youngest guys on the Black Jacks, had tackled the guy with the gun. By the time they were pulled apart, the boyfriend's buddy had a bullet in his chest and Rick had one in his side.

Sophie shuddered and cranked the heat up in the car. The thought of dealing with death, or near death, in a hospital, set her guts churning. Her face burned, but she had a small flutter of anticipation, knowing that Brody would be at the hospital too. At that moment, she allowed a tiny lick of hope to flare in her chest, before stuffing it down deep under plenty of reality checks. She touched her shirt over the scar hidden by it as a reminder of her previous misjudgment about men.

• • • •

CHAOS REIGNED AS ONE might expect at a big city hospital on an early Saturday morning. Sophie bitched her way past security, making several vain attempts to get someone to help her locate her group. Coming in through emergency probably wasn't the best plan, but she felt muddled, already spinning the gun shot soccer players story out in a thousand different ways and coming up with nothing good at the end of it.

After being shuttled between floors, she finally found Rafe and Metin, huddled around someone who looked like a surgeon. She braced herself against the wall as tidal waves of memory washed over her. Swallowing the urge to bolt, she noted how distressed both the coach and manager appeared by whatever the scrub-suited doctor in front of them was saying. She needed to rally. It was time to get a handle on this.

She set her shoulders and walked toward them. Both men seemed relieved to see her, which bolstered her. But she kept glancing around, seeking Brody. By the time she reached them, Metin had dropped into a seat.

Rafe pulled her aside. "He hates hospitals. You know his story, right?"

She stared at him, at a total loss. Metin Sevim's personal horror story had been news for months, not only in the sports world. She put a hand on Metin's shoulder and could feel him shivering.

Then, she spotted him. Brody, still dressed in the clothing she'd made him strip out of, then put back on when he'd pissed her off. She took a breath and had to acknowledge the fact that the sight of him made her knees unreliable. He stood, talking with someone else in scrubs, then spent a few minutes on the phone before looking at her. The relief in his eyes at that split second gave her another boost of confidence. She tried not to appear so obviously happy to see him, considering the circumstances.

"Hey." His calm voice jarred her, as if they had not spent an hour or so not long ago, naked, with her mouth-fucking and hand-jobbing him to climax, then kicking him out of her Dominatrix lair for no good reason.

She smiled, trying to keep it on a business level, but her heart did a painful tap dance in her chest and words caught in her throat.

"So, we need to contact their next of kin. I assume you have that info?" He dropped into a seat next to his coach, who still sat, shell-shocked and green around the edges.

She pointed to the slim briefcase slung over her shoulder. "Got everything here. Where can we go?"

Brody glanced up at the ceiling then leveled his gaze at her, giving her another jolt of surreal emotion. "I've arranged for a private room so we can all be on the call."

"Okay." She didn't see any point to delay. "Let's get this done." She blinked back tears and put a hand to her lips, embarrassed. Brody rose and put an arm around her and as if it was the most natural thing in the world, pulling her into a tight embrace.

"How are they?" she asked into his chest, hoping he'd never let her go.

Metin got to his feet. "Rick just got out of surgery. It's touch and go but the docs are optimistic. Nate's leg is broken all to hell." He stared at Brody. "What are we gonna do?"

Sophie looked from Metin's anguished face to Brody's, set in a stubborn way she'd never seen. Realization dawned. The Black Jacks had a long run of away games, a West Coast tour playing some of their league teams but ending with a crucial exhibition game against the Mexican national team. Something Metin had scheduled as a bit of a why the hell not? Before his star goalie had a concussion, of course. And well before his back-up keeper got shot in the leg while playing the hero.

"Oh, no you will not," she declared loudly. "I... I mean. He can't play." She pointed to Brody. "Surely you won't go now. You can't just leave these players here while you travel."

"Let's not talk about that now," Metin said, shoving his hands into his pockets. Rafe cleared his throat.

"C'mon." Brody guided her away from the group. "Let's get set up in the conference room and make these calls."

Rafe and Metin followed them, but they were all interrupted by a commotion from the opposite end of the hall. Parker, the team's captain, dashed down the hall, dragging Nicolas Garza with him. Brody frowned at the sight of them. Then he motioned for the men to join them in the stuffy, windowless room where they'd call two sets of parents to tell them that they, the people in charge of their sons, had not kept them safe from harm and now they were both lying in hospital fighting for their lives.

"What are we going to do about a keeper?" Nicco blurted out, bringing a nice level of awkward to the already tense room, while staring straight at Brody.

"Gee, Garza, not sure. Since you and your bullshit put Vaughn on ice." Rafe's tone made it clear how he felt about Nicco's sudden concern.

"We'll have to figure that out later. It's not a priority right now," Brody said with the sort of authority that shut everyone else up.

And with that, she understood that Robert J. Vaughn would be returning to his spot in goal within the week. The team needed him, medical advice be damned.

He leaned into her, his eyes intense. "It will be fine," he said, low-voiced, for her ears only.

She shivered. Had she spoken out loud? How did he know what she'd been thinking?

He touched her leg under the table, just a brush of skin, but in it he transferred the oddest sensation directly to her nervous system. A sudden calm settled over her brain, allowing her to focus. She had a job to do. Concentrating on the task at hand, she got to work, letting the legal side of her mind start anticipating questions from these players' agents and lawyers once they got past the parents.

Chapter Thirteen

When the team took the field for the last game on the grueling west coast tour, Brody had about convinced himself the whole concussion thing must be a bunch of alarmist nonsense from doctors worried about lawsuits. He'd never played better. Granted, he got headaches with predictable regularity, but he could coast through with painkillers and long stretches of sleep. The trainers evaluated him before and after every match, using the head injury protocol for acute concussion, and he always passed with flying colors.

The near lethal injuries of two of their own seemed to calm some of the roiling conflict between the pro-and anti-homosexual team member camps. Thank god for small favors.

Brody took practice shots while warming up for the final exhibition game. He had little hope they would do much more than hold their own against a strong Mexican side that had defeated the U.S. men's team twice already that year. But the Black Jacks were on a bit of a roll, having won every single match in their division, so hopefully they would carry some momentum into this day.

In spite of all the tragedy, hard work, grueling road trips, and newly annoying headaches, something soothing had settled over his psyche. It was the sort of peace he hadn't experienced since Nashville but one that had a decidedly different and healthier edge to it. Due in no small part to the fact he had struck up a nightly conversation with Sophie. His skin flushed thinking about her, how her tightly wound personality appealed to him, how hard she worked to prove her strength while yearning for someone to be strong for her at the same time.

He enjoyed their light flirty chatter, never actually touching on their one steamy encounter. Talking about news of the team, mostly. He anticipated it every day. It grounded him, pure and simple. He wasn't even sure what he wanted from her anymore other than having someone to talk to, to share things with. Although his wild, erotic dreams of her lithe, naked body kept his hand busy every night afterward. He was confident he'd put in the requisite ten thousand hours to consider himself a jack-off expert.

"Ow!" he yelped when a ball hit him in the chest. "Shit." He kicked the thing back out and focused on his day job.

• • • •

NICE SAVE. TOO BAD our forwards didn't convert.

Sophie's first chat message of the night brought a smile to his face. Wincing, he swallowed some painkillers and downed half a bottle of water before dropping into the chair. He was sick of hotels and this whole trip. The damn game had been close, right up until the last two or three minutes. He'd made an incredible save and set the midfield up for a great play, but their forward had stumbled, tripped by an opposing player which went unnoticed by the officials, effectively blowing the scoring opportunity.

The game had ended a 0-0 draw, which many Black Jack fans considered a victory if the social media chatter was to be believed. He, however, refused to accept tie games, believing them unfinished business unless settled by a shoot-out. But as a friendly exhibition, they'd agreed not to take it there, and all had shaken hands before exiting the field, exhausted and ready to go home.

A nervous, jittery energy coursed through him at the thought of seeing Sophie again. He had no way of understanding it, having spent nearly three years in service to a Mistress who had trained him as her perfect submissive: pliable, eager to please, needy while with Her, while remaining master of his destiny otherwise. He'd been turning over his experiences as a sub in his head lately and no longer believed it as clear-cut as that. He may have enjoyed getting off by learning to control his orgasm and how to please a woman, but something about the whole thing no longer felt right. As a matter of fact, it felt straight up sordid, tainted with the distance of time.

A surge of nausea he attributed to low blood sugar hit him as he typed out a reply.

Yeah. And how. Lazy fuckers.

Sophie: *I know you don't like games to end in a draw, but everyone seemed a little gassed. Probably could use the break.*

Brody: What's the latest with Rick and Nate? he asked, still trying to shake the low lying carsick feeling.

Sophie: *Rick's out of intensive care. His parents are with him. Nate's about to be released in a few days, with a lot of PT in his future plus a fistful of Vicodin. Speaking of which, how's the noggin?*

Brody: *Hurts today. Thinking I might have to do something drastic to distract myself.* He sat back, took deep breaths, as the dizzy sensation slowly faded.

Sophie: *Oh? Like what? Take a nap?*

Brody: *Maybe. After I take care of some personal business.*

He didn't know why he'd decided to take their usual friendly, informational exchange banter to a different level, but his ears buzzed with a distinct urge and the rest of him tingled in anticipation.

Sophie: *Personal, huh? Want some help?*

He grinned, pleased she hadn't shied away.

Her next words took some of the shine off that.

Sophie: *I mean, in a friendly sort of rub-down-after-a-hard-game way. Madame K says no charge for you.*

Brody: *I don't want Madame K.*

His phone buzzed immediately at his elbow. Sophie's number appeared on the screen, and he spent a few seconds staring at it, thinking he'd just ignore her and take that nap. But he didn't. He was better trained than that.

"Yes?" He reached under the towel for his cock which was diamond hard. Might as well finish what he started.

"Robert," she whispered. "Robert, you've been bad. I never came that night, you know. I don't like that, not a bit."

He drowned in her words, groaning at the last minute as the climax gripped his spine. He lay back, relaxed, but pissed off at the same time. He pressed the phone to his ear with his other hand.

"Thank you."

"My pleasure." She hung up before letting him return the favor, which he had fully intended to do. He glanced at the computer screen. Her chat icon showed her as offline.

"Goddamn you, Sophie." He got to his feet, then dropped face down on the bed, heading straight into a dreamless, restless sleep. He woke at two a.m., sweaty and breathless in the pitch black room.

He'd dreamed of his Mistress again, but instead of the beautiful savior he always took her for, she'd opened her robe to reveal a skeletal, burned carcass that lunged at him, forcing him to do things to her even as he swore he couldn't take another minute. Sitting up fast, the dizziness hit him hard. He stumbled for the bathroom and, after emptying his stomach, he crouched on the cool tile floor, legs clasped tight to his body.

He'd been such a fool. Would he ever have a normal relationship? Did he even know what that felt like? He'd been ignoring Kelli for so long he hoped she got the message, but even that seemed wrong. Why not Kelli, now that he had a better grasp on what had been done to him in college? Why not indeed?

Groaning, he leaned into the toilet to puke once more, hoping the demon he harbored would exit the same way, and leave him in peace.

I like it when you call me Robert, he said via text the next morning on the team bus to the airport.

Where did Brody come from, anyway? She replied as if they'd not ended their conversation the night before with a phone sex hand job for him and silence from her.

Brody: *Not sure. As long as I can remember, I've been Brody, although that makes for a bit of pain in the ass on legal docs. I do know one of my foster parents insisted on calling me Bobby Joe, which I fucking hated.*

Sophie: *Ah, so the J is for Joseph?*

Brody: *Yep. Good ol' Bobby Joe from the Tennessee hills, parentless, soccer-playing, straight-A student.*

Sophie: *I love your accent.*

He glanced around the bus at his teammates. Half of them were asleep wearing noise cancelling headphones, the other half were tapping messages on phones or small computers, likely doing their marketing-department-required social networking for the day. Which reminded him he hadn't logged onto any of his for over a week.

Another message from her arrived. *Were you treated badly in foster care?*

He took a breath, trying to decide how to relate that being shuttled around like a library book didn't exactly constitute being treated well. And how much he should tell her about the dirty apartments, often drunk or high parents, sometimes abusive temporary brothers, and the general unwanted feeling he still lugged around with him, no matter how far into adulthood he got.

Brody: *No. It was no fun, but nothing overtly abusive.* He shifted and winced when pain shot up from his shoulder into the base of his skull. That damn shoulder needed therapy. The head-cracker he'd gotten from Nicco and Cody had forced him to focus on the condition of his brain pain long enough to neglect the long-standing injury he had sustained when his Mistress had shackled him overnight, arms over his head, claiming he had failed to service her properly. An event he'd only half-remembered until that very moment.

God, she had really fucked with him. Those years were such a blur of intensity and discovery that he could only just now acknowledge as emotional and physical abuse. Only the briefest full memories would emerge now, as if he'd been chipping away at the wall holding them back, and they'd started to drip slowly into his consciousness. The shoulder thing he had chalked up to falling too many times on it in goal. But it had been her, his Mistress, who had bestowed that on him as punishment. And he had let her. A shiver shot down his spine.

Sophie: *Well, it must have been awful, not knowing where you'd be living month to month.*

He blinked at that. Then again, when she sent a second message on top of it:

I'm so sorry you had to go through it. It makes me mad, thinking of you as a little boy being tossed from house to house for the foster parent's monetary benefit.

Brody: *Yeah. Well, I turned out all right, I guess. It made me flexible, emotionally speaking.*

He wasn't even sure why he said such a thing, and wished he had the nerve to say what he wanted to right then. That it had been the worst sort of awful, and had left him with a giant, empty hole in the middle of his chest most days. Mainly because he had zero frame of reference for what it meant to have a healthy relationship with another person.

Sophie: *See you soon... Bobby Joe.*

Brody: *Don't even think about calling me that, Sophie Lynn.*

Sophie: *WTF? How did you... never mind. Safe trip.*

He smiled and typed his final message before he lost his nerve. *Since we're all friendly now to the point of phone sex, I wonder if we can we go out maybe to dinner or something when I get back?*

Her response was nearly instantaneous. *Probably not.*

He frowned when another message hit the screen. *Okay, Maybe.*

Taking that at face value, he settled into sleep, hoping to ward off the creeping onset of another headache.

Chapter Fourteen

It started when he hit the ground from the West Coast tour. She realized this as she opened her front door to discover a delivery boy clutching two-dozen red roses and a note:

I won't give up until you let me buy you dinner, RJV

She scoffed and sent him a chat message informing him of her rose allergy, but assuring him the ladies in the front office enjoyed the flowers. He ignored her a solid three days after that. Once she got over being impressed at his self-control, she forced away any sort of silly girlie giddiness at the thought of a man sending her flowers.

Hope equaled a recipe for disappointment, she reminded herself, touching her scar through her clothes nearly a hundred times a day, keeping that mantra going. She had loved Frank, the supposed man of her dreams. And he'd been a lying, stealing SOB who had, in the end, nearly killed her. No, she would not go out with Robert Joseph Vaughn. She simply couldn't afford to risk her soul that way.

She had a Madame Katrina session scheduled for Saturday, so she donned her usual garb and attitude and earned an easy thousand bucks. It had been a fairly predictable session, which was a relief. Although part of her wished it had been Brody. Her disappointment when she spotted her not-Brody client made punishing the guy the way he requested that much easier.

"Yo, that guy said he'll be back next weekend." Dante tossed her a towel when she emerged from the shower at two in the morning. "Nice work, Kat."

"Yeah," she said, still a little wobbly coming down off her own Domme high. She did enjoy it. But the memory of Brody's words spoken in that knee-melting, syrupy accent: I want to make love to you, Sophie, wafted across her brain. Damned men. She had to purge him. Big time.

"I got a scary email from Frank," she said as casually as possible, tugging her hair up into a ponytail.

Dante's eyes narrowed. "Oh?"

"Yeah, so just be aware that if I text you 911, it's a Frank sighting."

"Sure." He kept it simple, but there was power in that word. Dante would never let Frank hurt her.

"Thanks." She gave him a hug, and he hung onto her for a few extra seconds as reassurance.

• • • •

ON SUNDAY SHE SLEPT in, relishing the rest, but missed her Brody fix. Even if it were only the sound of his voice or the sight of his words on her phone screen. The doorbell rang at noon, surprising her as she finished up some laundry. She'd been pondering whether to read or watch a movie while eating a pint of ice cream and had discovered she had nothing worthwhile in her freezer.

She opened her front door without thinking and came face to face with a delivery kid holding a small cooler. He consulted a piece of paper, then handed the cooler to her. A small truck with the words Washtenaw Dairy emblazoned on the side, her favorite local ice cream place, was parked on the street. Unable to suppress a grin, she opened the cooler to find three pints of her favorites, including Double Mackinac Island fudge. She found a small envelope tucked down between the containers.

Round two: What? Me? Bribing you with your favorite treat. Yes. That's me. Dinner? Monday? RJV

Sophie opened her laptop and sent him an email, a slower method of delivery than their usual text messages, but she wanted to put her carefully considered thoughts into words. As she composed the message, she ate his gift of ice cream, letting delicious bites melt in her mouth and slide down her throat.

Dear RJV

Thanks for your valiant efforts, especially with the ice cream. Good job remembering my one vice after too much coffee.

I think that you and I need to ponder carefully whether we should see each other socially. I'm not sure I'm ready to date, and you really ought to focus on women closer to your age. I enjoy being your friend. And it would be sad if our friendship faded because I won't go out on a date with you.

So the answer is still no. But thank you,

SLH

She hit send and turned the thing off, then got lost in a day of classic movies and dessert.

• • • •

AFTER THAT, SHE WAS on the receiving end of the silent treatment for a solid two weeks. When he finally emerged, sort of by accident, into her line of vision, she'd been reduced to a twitchy, pissed off mess, with no one but herself to blame.

Frank had indeed been sending her emails, and he'd even called once, leaving a message she deleted before listening to a single word. She should call the police, but she notified Dante instead.

She'd been sitting on her office ledge sipping an afternoon decaf latte and enjoying the Brody view from afar. She made it a point to watch the team practices, always willing him not to work so hard, not to leap for balls and put his head so near the feet, knees, and skulls of other players. Being a near-professional Brody-stan, she knew Kelli had faded. Her photo hadn't appeared anywhere near his online presence for weeks, and she'd heard through the grapevine the girl had been making a bit of a fool of herself, hanging around, begging Brody to pay attention to her.

"But for the grace of god... or something," she muttered, half sympathetic with the poor girl who no longer got her way with the sexy soccer star. Just as she went back to work, a hulking presence appeared in her doorway. She glanced up on autopilot, assuming the man there had come from marketing with some reports she'd requested.

"Sophie, my sweet, my darling, just look at you."

Her blood froze at the sound of his voice. She gulped, and her knees trembled, but she stayed upright. "Get out of here, Frank, or whatever the fuck your name is." Her voice sounded strong. A good thing, since her brain had locked up in terror. Just the sight of him sent her programmed body into overdrive, forcing her to fight the urge to drop to her knees and crawl toward him the way she used to do. The distinct sound of her door closing and the snick of the lock made tears burn the backs of her eyes.

"Oh, I'm just stopping by to check on you. To see what you've made of yourself." He ran his hand along the top of a leather chair. She gritted her teeth with the urge to pour bleach over the damn thing.

"I'm calling security." She picked up the phone, but her head clanged, and her ears buzzed with a sickeningly familiar refrain of submit! Be cowed and be rewarded! At that split second, she recalled the security call button located under her desk could be activated without his knowledge. So she put the phone back down while keeping her gaze on him, watching for danger.

His control over her, even after all she'd been through, fascinated and terrified her in equal measure. Not surprising, since he'd spent nearly two years grooming her in ways she still didn't understand. His gray gaze pinned her like an ant, or a mouse. That flipped a switch in her head, rallying inner forces she didn't realize she possessed. She refused to be a victim, no matter how strong the compulsion at that moment to drop to the floor and beg him to fuck her.

Keeping her grip on the phone, she took a step to the left, putting her foot within reach of the alarm button. She cursed herself for recalling his lips on her skin, for remembering the sting of his palm, sometimes harsh with a smack to her ass, other times to her face when she made too much noise while they had sex. So firm, yet smooth. So comforting and gentle as he guided her through a door, or up a flight of steps, anywhere in public, many times in private, which was part of her conditioning. She clenched her jaw, forcing the sensory-overloading memories away.

As soon as she opened them, Frank loomed into her space, his tall frame towering over her. She tried to meet his gaze, gave it all she had, but her training took hold and wouldn't allow it. She kept her gaze averted as his palm touched her face, tender now, his voice a smooth, deep rumble. She leaned into him while trying to maintain her foot's pressure on the floor alarm without giving away her action.

"Now, now, dear one. My best girl, my Sophie. You haven't forgotten, have you? How you are when you're with me?" His words lit a flame in her gut, and she responded by rote.

"No. S-s-s-sir," she said, eyes still lowered.

He rubbed her arm, tugging her ever closer, whispering like he always had. Calming her nerves before the storm, but drawing her away from the alarm, which she wasn't certain had been activated.

"Look at me," he demanded, gripping her arm tight, now that their bodies touched. She sensed his erection, that giant, intimidating dick he'd used against her, but sometimes for her. Which she'd let him do, all the while convinced he had her best interests at heart.

She shook her head, balling her hands into fists. Pulse pounding, heart racing, gut turning over, she kept her gaze on the floor. The slap sent her reeling backward, tripping over her heels. But it didn't surprise her. Frank loved smacking her around, always under the guise of necessary discipline.

She would forget his shirts at the laundry, and he would smile, pour her a glass of wine, help with dinner. Then later, in the bedroom, he would rip her clothes off and smack her face repeatedly, his own face never betraying a lick of emotion. After leaving her alone to ponder her laziness, he'd return, flip her over on her stomach, and fuck her without preamble or pretext. And she would let him.

Because the next morning he'd get up, fix her breakfast, and feed it to her, then set the food aside and bring her to a shuddering, yelling climax with his talented fingers and tongue. This passed as acceptable behavior for years. She'd been weakened by her brush with Evan Adams, had pushed him away from her and then whirled around to find Frank. So she continued thinking that he was The One. Until she found herself alone on Dexter-Ann Arbor Road with one leg pinned under a Harley and fighting for her life. That's when shit got real.

"Get out, Frank, before security gets here."

She made sure her voice remained free of fear or anger. Frank hated it when she got hysterical for any reason. If she showed anything more than a bare minimum of normal human reaction, he'd punish her for it. For being unhappy over something at work or pissed off at the news of the world. He considered it his job to keep her calm and free from emotion other than those he demanded of her. And he did, too, smoothing off every single rough edge she possessed until she became polished like a stone at the bottom of a river and with just as much motivation to live. Oh, and minus a spleen, a kidney, and enduring a year of punishing physical therapies so she could walk like a normal person.

She turned, putting the door behind her, hoping to move toward it and escape. He kept coming at her, his lips pulled away from his teeth in a feral grimace. He seemed well put together in a suit and shiny shoes, but something loomed under his surface, a sort of naked desperation. The man reeked of it. She used that to give her courage and to fuel her next words.

"You are a class-A, walking, talking douche bag posing as a man. You're nothing more than an abusive rapist and a useless waste of my time."

That stopped him. His eyes clouded over, sending a spike of primal fear through her body. She had taken a calculated risk, but a plan emerged, one that would only work if she had managed to trip the security alarm. She needed witnesses. No one believed her when she tried to tell them stories of her allowing this man to bind her arms and legs, to drop hot wax on her bare skin, to clamp her nipples so hard they were distended for days. No one bought her story that she believed him to be a faker and abuser. She had allowed some level of abuse for so long, she no longer had validity when she claimed it.

Using every ounce of terror-tinged energy she possessed, she stepped in front of him. "That's right, Sir." She spit the word out. Then spit directly at him, her saliva dripping down his dark, stubbled cheek. That face she'd adored for so long that had crushed her soul in every way possible. "Fuck you...Sir." She reached back to unlock the door. He acted according to type, backhanding her so hard her body hit the door with the full force of the blow.

The crunching sensation in the middle of her face forced a scream from her throat when his fingers gripped her hair and yanked her to her feet. Nose throbbing, she struggled to breathe. Her high-heeled shoes scrabbled against the floor while he dragged her backwards. Something cold touched her neck. A knife? Fear bloomed in her chest, darkening her vision.

"Shut up, cunt," he growled. "You were about as useful to me as a blow-up doll with a couple of holes in it." He shook her, ripping the hair from her head and pressing the knife close. "Give me the money in the safe. Now."

She sobbed, tried to suck in a breath, but flooded her sinuses and throat with blood. "Safe?" she managed, trying to shy away from his blade. Her mind spun. What safe?

"Don't lie to me, bitch." He looked away from her, toward the door, and a sinister smile spread over his face. "Well, hello there. Who do have we here?"

Sophie attempted to focus her streaming eyes on the man standing at the now-open door, dressed in the Black Jacks practice gear, his hands clenched into fists, flanked by the security guards. "Brody, get back. Don't...ow...ow!"

Frank tightened his grip, and a sting at her neck indicated he'd nicked her skin. "Is this your handsome young boy toy, my dearest? I know you are ever so fond of these youngsters. You really are getting on a bit, a little dried up perhaps, for this stud?"

Brody stepped into the room. "Let her go. The police are on their way," he said, his voice calm.

Frank laughed so loud she sensed it deep in her soul, along with the conviction that this could be her final moments on earth. He fully intended to kill her right in front of these men.

"Let me give you some advice about this bitch." He gave her a shake. "She's hardly worth your effort, trust me. Sniveling, whining, and useless and... oof."

The air left Frank's lungs in a loud whoosh, filling Sophie's ear with the sound and heat of it. Released, she dropped to her knees, sobbing and spluttering, crawling towards the security guards who grabbed her and hustled her to her feet.

Brody had come at him like a torpedo, barreling into his chest without regard to the fact he had a knife to her neck. They rolled across her office floor, fists flying. But Frank quickly learned a hard truth—that there were not many men in the world in as good a shape as Brody Vaughn. He had the asshole pinned with both arms yanked up behind his back in minutes.

The guards pulled Frank up and Brody ran to her, barely breathing hard, and holding out his arms. She tried to stay upright and let him hold her, but when the room faded, she let it, willing Brody to catch her before she hit the floor again.

Chapter Fifteen

Brody sat in his car, gathering his thoughts and courage. For as long as he lived, he would remember that scene, that freak show asshole hanging onto Sophie's hair, her shattered nose streaming blood, the glint of a knife at her porcelain throat. A beast had risen in his chest, filling him with strength and wildness he didn't know he possessed. He'd attacked, nothing in him but the urge to get his woman away from the crazy man who was hurting her.

His woman.

He shook his head and gripped the steering wheel a bit longer. She'd mentioned a mistake in her past to him, nothing more. He'd had no idea it involved an insane stalker. Taking a long, deep breath, he got out, then forced more air into his lungs.

After spending a restless night in the hospital being monitored for her own concussion, Sophie had gone home, claiming to be fine and needing to be alone. So he'd left her that way for a total of two days, then greeted her at her office on her first day back with a cup of coffee and a smile.

"So, now that you owe me, I'll ask you again. But you can pick the date venue."

She'd sighed, touched the bandage covering her nose. He'd tried hard not to flinch at the ugly bruising around her eyes. That bastard—he should have killed him.

"Okay, I give," she said. His heart lifted, teasing him with a quick tremor of happiness. Unable to resist, he put a soft kiss on her forehead and left after confirming she'd come up with her dream date and text him later.

But now, after all that effort, he was having gut-churning second thoughts. He wanted something else, Madame Katrina perhaps, not the Sophie who exuded her power along with a vulnerability that pulled him in odd directions. He had no intention of doing anything more than exactly as she specified. Dinner at Vineology, which was some restaurant in Ann Arbor, then a concert at The Ark, although he had no idea what that meant. She claimed to have tickets for a nationally known blues band there. No nightcaps at her place or his, no random groping. Nothing. Just the two of them talking, enjoying food and drink and music, getting to know each other. His pulse raced no matter how many tricks he used to calm it.

Get a grip, man. It's a date. Jesus. Not a marriage ceremony.

He walked up the steps to the porch of her bungalow-style house, body tensing with anxiety. The door swung open when he touched his knuckles to it. But he stayed on the threshold, calling out for her. She emerged, a smaller white bandage on her nose, the bruising faded but still there. But to him, she appeared as Venus, like all the most perfect women in the universe, rolled into one short, brown-haired, blue-eyed package. He sucked in a breath.

She touched the bandage and flushed deep red. "I must look like shit," she said, her voice nasally and low.

"You are a vision." He held out a hand, a natural-seeming gesture, and one that he hadn't planned or anticipated.

She put her palm in it, and he tugged her close without thinking too much about it. But never more sure about anything at the same time. Once she was close, he tilted her chin up and kissed both her cheeks, and then her forehead, and finally her lips. Keeping it gentle, he probed with his tongue, so revved he wanted to toss her on the bed and have her right then. But he wanted her to set the pace. He sensed her relax, going up on her tiptoes to reach him and wrap her arms around his neck. It didn't feel like a first kiss. He honestly believed he had been kissing her forever.

He broke it off. "Sorry, but if we do much more of that, we'll definitely miss our reservation and the concert at The Boat."

She cocked her head at him, then threw her head back and laughed. Breathless at the sight of her long, lean neck and unable to stop, he touched his lips there, just under her jaw line. At the connection, meant only as a simple caress, she gasped and molded into him, giving him more access and tossing him right over the precipice.

"Where's the damn bedroom?" he asked, picking her up and kissing every inch of her face and neck.

"Straight back." Sophie, his Sophie, sighed into his skin. "Hurry up."

"I am," he said, never meaning anything more.

He stumbled, stepping out of his shoes on the way toward the back of the house and found the room, neat as a pin, the bed covered with decorative pillows. She kept whispering his name, clinging to him as if her life depended on it, and somewhere between her living room and bedroom, Brody's heart collapsed in on itself. He shed the weak submissive and grew into a new skin, one where he would bring the pleasure, at his pace, to his woman.

He eased her back, unzipping her dress and sliding it off her shoulders, kissing every centimeter of skin as he revealed it. God, she tasted so delicious, so warm and tempting, like a cup of hot vanilla tea or a shot of hundred-year-old bourbon. His body throbbed, aching for a connection. When she lay there, naked and utterly still, he stood and slipped out of his slacks and shirt. Something stopped him, as the whole scene drifted off center all of a sudden.

She propped up on her elbows, one eyebrow raised, and stared right at his straining underwear. "What is it? What's wrong?"

He discarded his last article of clothing, unable to keep from shaking, loving the way she looked at him, but terrified of it at the same time. His Mistress had done that a lot—got him hard enough to cut diamonds, then forced him to sit or stand, naked, without speaking while she glared at him. She'd touch and tease every inch of him before he would be allowed to do or say anything else.

He froze, unable to breathe, his long conditioning and Sophie's naturally dominant personality rendering him immobile.

"Robert," she said again, reaching out her hand. He took it and let her pull him back onto the bed. "Make love to me. Please, I need you to."

He nodded, but still trembled, on the knife edge of a panic attack.

She leaned back on a stack of pillows and drew him down to her. "It's fine. Don't fret. We're both so fucked up." She sucked in a breath, and he sensed anger in her then. "What happened to you? Who made you do this?" She touched his neck. The tattoo that had, at one time, meant more to him than his own living heart muscle, but now seemed like a childish, futile gesture, meaning exactly nothing to the woman he'd honored it with. It seemed to pulse between them.

He let Sophie hold him until their breathing calmed, then rolled over onto his back and stared at her ceiling. She scooted down next to him, propped up on her elbow, her fingers tracing across all his body art. "What are the letters on your back?" she asked, brushing his biceps with her lips.

"Initials," he said, closing his eyes, loving her touch on him, wishing like hell he could close the deal, give her what they both wanted. But something kept him from it. And the blame for that lay at the feet of one woman. "Mine and...." He swallowed hard, forcing his throat to make the sound he required. "Hers. My Mistress. We were together for nearly three years. I loved her, I think. Or at least I loved what she did for me. Or rather, what I thought she did."

He pulled her close to his bare chest. "But now, I'm not sure she didn't use my body without a ton of concern for the rest of me. That hurts," he choked out, face burning and gut aching. "A lot." He tried to sit up, but she hung onto him, firm, with just enough pressure to let him know he wouldn't be allowed to run from her.

"I know." She continued to trace the floral patterns on his pecs with her fingernail. "I never got a physical tattoo. The one he etched into my brain sufficed."

Brody gazed down at her, his heart thumping at the memory of her in that asshole's clutches. He wiped her tears. "That guy in your office?"

She nodded and tucked back into his torso. They stayed quiet for a while, each sunk deep in the mire of their own thoughts, histories, and mistakes. She continued to move her palm across his abs until she moved lower and found her target. He shifted, exhaling at her sweet grip, but then plucked it off and rolled so she lay on her back, and he was propped up on one elbow next to her.

"My turn, Sophie Lynn," he said softly and lowered his mouth to hers, entangling with her tongue. The scary, pre-programmed sensations still thrummed through him, but something stronger had taken over in his brain. He moved lower, teasing her nipples to hard peaks. He kept going, nibbling her stomach, tracing that horrific scar with a fingertip and his tongue.

When he slipped between her legs, she had her hips tilted, her sex exposed to him. That moment of trust hit him square in the gut. After all she'd been through, she had zero reason for that, but yet, there she lay, open and vulnerable—for him.

He traced the outer edges of her pink flesh, teased the small nub emerging from its hood, loving the lusty scent of turned-on female. He sighed with satisfaction and a small tremor of relief. Nothing revved him up more than watching a woman's body ready itself for him. But the sensations surging through him were like nothing he'd ever experienced or imagined he might.

Shaking, he lowered his mouth to taste her. She twisted her fingers in his hair, her voice loud in his ears, begging, pleading with him in a way that nearly sent him straight over the edge. Her response to his lips and fingers was immediate and exquisite.

"Yes!" she cried, moving her hips, as the rich musk of aroused woman swirled in his head and her pussy gripped his fingers.

She flopped back, gasping for breath. He crawled up to face her, his entire body trembling but with a sort of joyous, almost-perfect emotion, one that frightened him, and gave him purpose.

"I don't have protection," he choked out, ready to expire if he didn't get inside her soon. "But I always wear it, I mean... you know... oh, holy hell, Sophie." He groaned when she angled her body, grabbed him with both legs, and drew him in.

"Ah... Brody," she whispered, enveloping him with her whole self, the wondrous moment coalescing in her eyes. He went deep, then pulled out, just for the experience of entering her again, never taking his gaze from hers.

"Come inside me." She arched her back. "Come with me. I know you want it, Robert." Using just enough of her Domme voice to make him do exactly that, fast, without a shred of control. Instead of pissing him off like it did with Kelli, he reveled in it, owned it, and filled her, crying her name. Their bodies moving together in the oldest dance known to humankind.

"I love you," he whispered into her neck, meaning it.

"I know," she said, still holding him close.

They must have slept, because by the time a noise jolted him awake, the strange bedroom had darkened. Panic hit his chest, but when he saw the sheet-covered form to his left, his heart ceased its pounding and he laid back down, curling around Sophie's body and sighing into her hair.

"We missed The Boat concert."

She shifted and pressed back against him. "It's The Ark, you goof." Her voice sounded fuzzy with sleep.

"Whatever," he said, running one hand up to cup her breast and the other down to tease between her legs. "Mmm.... I was gonna say I'm hungry, let's eat, but...."

"Me too. Let's get up."

She reached back to tug at his hair as he tweaked a nipple and felt her body respond from to tip to toe.

"Okay then, this is us. Getting up." He nibbled her neck and shoulder. She made a noise between a groan and a sigh. "Show me, Sophie." He used a low, commanding voice, like his coach-on-the-field one. Something he'd never done in a sexual situation. It buzzed around in his ears and brought a distinct tingle to his skin. "Come, baby. Now."

He bit her shoulder again, stroking her while the glorious, incandescent orgasm rolled off her in waves. He loved how they both shivered with the force of it. "Damn," he said into her neck.

"Truer word never spoken." Rolling all the way over to pin him, she climbed up to straddle his hips in one fluid motion. She smiled down at him, a wicked gleam in her eyes. His automatic reaction to the position—that of cowering inside his own brain as he used to do when his Mistress would ride him, smacking his hips and tugging the nipple clamp chain while he bit down on the urge to blow or at least touch her—didn't happen. Instead, he grinned and thrust up. Her body enveloped him, and they both sighed with pleasure.

"Come down here," he said, his voice croaky. "Kiss me."

She dropped forward, curtaining them, shutting out the world with her thick brown hair. He met her halfway, digging his fingers into her hips before tearing his lips from hers to latch onto a nipple. She squealed with delight, moved faster and faster, until he couldn't hold back.

"God," he groaned into her breasts. "Gonna come."

She gave his nipple a hard pinch. A decidedly animal-sounding noise emerged from his throat, and he let himself have it, coming and coming until he could barely breathe. He blinked up at the ceiling, dazed, and hungrier than he'd ever been in his life.

She stayed astride him, running her hands across his tats. He blew out a breath when she lifted off him and flopped down to his side with a sigh.

"You are pretty good at this, aren't ya?" She framed it as less a question, more a declaration, while their heartbeats slowed to normal rhythms.

"So I'm told." He stretched and pulled her close, panic settling into his chest.

He didn't want to go. He wanted to stay there with her forever. Impractical, but typical, given how many times his Mistress would allow him to stay, only to boot him out, sometimes naked, onto her back lawn, saying he needed a reality check about how clingy he'd become. He shivered as that vision hit him. Another escapee from the repressed memory bank he'd labeled The Nashville Years.

As if sensing his tension, Sophie kissed him softly, then got up and headed for the bathroom. She emerged wearing a robe and a grin. "Starving?"

He nodded and got up, grateful she didn't press him on what he'd been thinking about, but still wobbly at the thought of having to go home to his own house and leave her behind.

"C'mon Robert." She held out a hand. He took a deep breath, and grasped it, recognizing that move now—something that signaled a next step for them both. "I make a mean stack of pancakes."

Chapter Sixteen

Sophie sat at her usual perch in her office, high above the action, while the team went through its paces before starting a long stretch of matches. They had three in a row on their home pitch, then were headed South to play in Texas and Georgia. Brody tried, with his usual pleasantly convincing techniques, to get her to travel with them. She'd demurred, still not comfortable with full public acknowledgement of their relationship after six months of essentially hibernating with him at her house during the team's off-season. People probably knew about them, but she wanted to keep it private, just between them a bit longer. Brody had other ideas, those of the polar opposite sort, which had become a sore point between them.

So, she anticipated their brief break with a positive attitude. She'd managed to convince him that, just because she didn't want him to move in with her, it didn't mean she didn't care about him. The poor guy had been through a lot of his crucial development years without anyone to truly love him. She understood what he needed.

Plus, she suspected she did love him, which terrified her. So she held back a part of her for reasons she didn't fully understand, which had led to a few strange, low-key arguments, leaving them both unhappy for days at a time. The nature of their dynamic didn't allow for much disagreement, as both of them wanted so badly to please the other. Their psycho-sexual programming proved hard to break outside the bedroom as well as in it.

She brought it up to him once, but he scoffed and said if an argument was what she wanted, he'd be happy to oblige her. She'd smacked his arm, accused him of patronizing her, doing all she could to goad him into a healthy, air-clearing disagreement. He kissed his way out of it, kissing her all over in his typical way. But it bugged her, and she didn't understand why. They had a long way to go if their relationship was to be truly healthy, which was why the upcoming club-enforced separation felt well-timed. She planned to suggest that they see a therapist together once he returned. His willingness to do that with her would go a long way towards her decision about moving in together.

She could barely repress a grin at the sight of him, her man, her Robert, as she called him in her house and nowhere else. Her very own god-among-men out there, tall, fit, talented, imposing. Recalling how he'd allowed her to use ropes the night before, binding him lightly, and blindfolding him, teasing him until he hit a fever pitch and had his shut-down moment. Then she'd ripped off all his bonds and the eye cover. They'd stared at one another for a few seconds before she said, "Now, take what you want."

Which he had, in such a primal way, she still shivered with the memory of it. Going Full Domme didn't appeal to her with him. He required a blend of her full heart, along with some of the play, or he'd likely tip back over into that bizarre, half-frozen state he'd pulled their first time. That bitch in Nashville had done a number on him. And Sophie would love to get her hands on the woman. But Brody insisted he didn't ever want to see her or to make peace in his soul by confronting her. So she had to respect that.

As she watched, the team divided up for the end of practice scrimmage. Nicco squared off against the asshole homophobe. Sophie's heart raced, recalling the last time that had happened. But things seemed fine. At least at first.

She hated the way Metin allowed the scrimmages to get so physical and the way Brody never stepped back from them, even knowing he had to be careful not to hurt his head again. His headaches had started fading, which he attributed to getting satisfactorily laid on a regular basis. But she'd done her research on concussion, and going completely contrary to doctor's orders and playing so soon was a bold—read: stupid—move on his part. She stood, assuming that the usual melee of masculine aggression that concluded all of their practices would not end with any injuries.

Her phone beeped—the private one. She frowned. She'd told Dante she was taking a few weeks off. Brody had been making some noise about wanting her to stop all that Madame Katrina bullshit, as he put it. She nipped that in the bud, telling him in no uncertain terms he had zero say about that part of her life.

Finding a replacement for Madame K would be a delicate business. She didn't trust many women to keep their mouths shut about potentially well-known clients. Dante sent her a text to say the woman they'd vetted for a month had agreed to be interviewed, if she were still interested. He didn't get Sophie's sudden disinterest in the job, unable to imagine why she'd stop until she asked him if his lover would be overjoyed if he took on the Dom role with a bunch of needy gay subs.

"You've got a boyfriend? Finally! That is awesome!"

"Shut up." She'd flushed with embarrassment. But she liked the sound of the word.

Just as she composed her message back to him, a loud shout from below caught her attention. She rushed to the window, heart in her throat. A group of players were gathered around the goal. She dropped the phone and ran down to the field, shoving her way through. The players moved out of the way for her this time. Nothing ever remained a secret for very long in an organization like this.

"Robert." She used her best commanding wake up now voice, crouching next to him. "What the fuck happened?" she demanded to the legs forming a cage around them. Metin appeared at her shoulder.

"Nothing. He just dropped. I swear it," the coach said. "No one touched him or was even anywhere near him." She rose, in a daze, as the paramedics loaded him into an ambulance that had pulled out onto the pitch. Metin pushed her. "Go with him."

She gripped Brody's ice-cold hand as they intubated him. His eyes never once opened. Tears dropped onto the sheet as she stared at his slack face. "Robert," she breathed. Then, as a last resort, she prayed.

• • • •

AFTER A FEW HOURS OF observation, Brody blinked and woke.

"I'm thirsty," he whispered.

Sophie scrambled to her feet, got him water, and brought back a nurse. The woman ran his vitals, asked him questions about who he was, what day it was, the year, the city. He got all the answers right, drinking two huge cups of water in the meantime.

"Hurts," he gasped, leaning back and putting his arm over his face. "Can we dim the lights or something?"

She glanced up at the nurse, scared, seeking words of reassurance. None came. Just "I'll get the doctor," and a quick disappearance. Metin and Rafe hovered outside the door. She gestured at them to come in. Brody slipped into sleep, mumbling, shifting around, the only way she realized he wasn't unconscious again. She knew how restlessly he slept.

"He shouldn't be playing." She glared at the men.

"I'm trying to find someone new. It's not easy." Rafe ran a hand down his face.

Brody mumbled and tried to roll over. She put her lips to his ear, whispered soothing words as she sometimes did in their bed at night, calming him when he got trapped between awake and asleep. The doctor came in, trailing pessimism like a noxious cloud.

"We have to get another CAT scan," he said to a nurse. "He keeps drifting off. That's not good." He made a notation on his tablet computer.

Her face flame hot with fury. "Not good? That's a medical term?" She remained next to Brody. "Can we be a tad more specific? We're all grownups here."

The doctor sighed and looked at her. "It's likely that the old concussion never fully healed. His brain is probably swelling now and pressing against his skull. All the recent symptoms you told me about, and what I hear from today's incident, points to that fact. This is, in a word, bad."

The doctor held up a hand.

"Excuse me, I have to get this order in. You can stay with him until he goes up for the test," he said to the room before he left.

• • • •

BY THE TIME HE GOT wheeled back to his room at midnight, Brody was awake, alert, and starving. Sophie nearly passed out from relief and started bossing the staff around to get him some food. She sat near his head, hand on his arm, both of them in their respective cocoons of silence, waiting for the meal to show.

"I have to play," he said, not in any firm way. "I don't know anything else."

She understood that he meant it. But instead of arguing, she stayed quiet while he devoured the food and downed almost a gallon of water. The words "not good" swirled around in her tired brain. Finally falling asleep in the recliner, she woke only when a nurse draped a blanket over her.

The morning brought news she didn't expect. The doctors declared that while Brody's brain showed signs of recent trauma, there was no swelling at all. They had no explanation for his loss of consciousness but advised strongly against taking any risk that he might jar his spine or neck or skull for the next eight to ten months. He'd burst out laughing, got out of bed, and asked for his clothes. Her heart sank, but she handed him the jeans and shirt she'd brought and drove him home.

"Coming up?" he asked mildly as she sat, the car still running, in the parking lot under his condo building.

She glanced at him, her heart shredded, and her ingrained self-preservation tendencies kicking in big time. "No." She kept it light. "I have a doctor's appointment in Ann Arbor tomorrow morning. You should get a shower and get some rest."

Running her hand down his stubbly face, she tried hard not to put much behind the gesture. Despite her gut deep need to stay with him, there, anywhere, she forced a smile, gritting her teeth. He gave her an odd look, then climbed out of her car and came around to the driver's side window. Lowering it, she smiled at his handsome face.

She loved him. She knew it. But the whole medical thing freaked her out. How could she allow herself to love this man only to get bitch-slapped by karma?

He touched a fingertip to her nose, and then walked to the elevator, leaving her to stew, steam, worry, fret, and freak out all in the space of about ten seconds. Throwing the car in reverse, she left. She did have an appointment, a routine check-up, and thought a night away from him might settle her nerves a little. Until she got home and touched her face, surprised to find she'd been crying.

Chapter Seventeen

Brody sat in the trainer's room after his first practice back. The man worked his sore shoulder, chattering away about some league gossip he barely heard. His head hurt so badly, it consumed him, as if nothing in the world existed but pain. He literally, at that moment, could see stars, stripes, birdies, and everything in between, like a cartoon character after getting whomped with an anvil.

But he'd be fine. He had to be fine. He had to play. Their final stretch of fall season friendlies were coming up, and the team was on the verge of breaking through in a big way. As the only goalkeeper available, he simply had no choice. His innate competitiveness served him well. No one would replace him.

He must have made a sound. The trainer stood in front of him as he tried to focus and failed. He listed to the left and dropped onto the hard table. By the time the trainer had brought Metin running, he'd bounced back up, standing, stretching, and ignoring the way sounds were sort of echo-like.

"What? I'm fine. I just needed food and some painkillers."

The coach had a vise grip on his arm, his dark face stuck up close to Brody's. "Vaughn," the man ground out. "You are not okay. I can tell. I have to call in a transfer."

"No." He yanked out of Metin's grasp. "I'm good. Just need to eat and take some aspirin." The trainer raised an eyebrow at the coach. Brody's ears burned. "Cut the crap, you guys. I'm fine. No transfers," he said to Metin. "I mean it. This is my goddamn spot. I earned it."

Metin nodded and walked out. Another goalie had been brought in at a high cost during the spring trade season. And that replacement asshole would not be getting anywhere near Brody's goal. No fucking way. Even as he thought this, the room did a sudden alarming tilt. He gripped the wall, grimacing, thinking about Sophie, how much he needed her. But she'd been busy lately, working and sorting out her Dominatrix replacement, all the while ignoring the hell out of him.

He didn't get her sometimes. Especially that whole we-don't-argue-enough nonsense. What a crazy thing to claim. They were happy together. And he was within a hairsbreadth of asking her to marry him. Something he never in a zillion years imagined doing with anyone.

Her slow, determined thawing of his inner submissive had brought out a side of him he never realized he possessed. They now embraced their mutual fetish without shame or fear. He'd even turned the tables on her once or twice, to their mutual satisfaction.

No Dominant existed in their relationship. But things were capital H-O-T. Full of the kind of kinky bondage and ass-smacking they both appreciated without it going too far in either direction. He loved it. And her. So her current chilly silence drove him insane, even though he was determined to respect it.

He stumbled to his locker and then to the showers, the eerie echo of the sounds magnified by the large, tiled room. Nicco and Parker were talking to Metin when he emerged, the rest of the team having faded after the arduous practice.

The thump-thump of his heartbeat reverberated in his skull so loudly he had to sit and take long breaths to avoid throwing up. His mantra repeated in a loop: nausea? Not good. Constant headaches? Not good. Dizziness and echoes in your ears? Not good. Not good. Not. Fucking. Good.

His phone screen showed a number of messages, texts, team updates, and other random shit. But nothing from Sophie. He drove home in a daze, determined not to call her. He knew it was good for him. The way she forced him to be without her on occasion. He didn't like it, but he humored her.

He never tired of her company, but he had to face his own demons that made him antsy and unhappy when they were apart. He would stay with her as much as she allowed, and she'd stayed at his place a few times. But she always withdrew to her private space, forcing him to cope with the fact that she hadn't left him. She just needed time alone.

He parked, walked to the elevator, and hit the up button, realizing too late that there was no food in his fridge. He should have stopped, but that would've taken way too much energy. Maybe he could scrounge something before sleeping, one thing he did a lot lately.

Once inside, he dropped his keys on a side table and inhaled the most glorious scent imaginable. As a professional athlete, he required a lot of calories to match his daily output of energy, but lately seemed to have lost his taste for food, which really sucked because he loved to eat almost as much as he loved to fuck.

"Hey," he called out, relieved beyond measure that she'd somehow read his mind, and his caloric depletion. She was here, making dinner for him. At the sight of her, dressed in dark jeans and a team-labeled sweatshirt, he smiled, stepped over to her, and picked her all the way up, kissing her the entire time.

She spluttered and protested, "Get off me. I'm cooking."

"Cook later. Fuck now," he declared, carrying her out of the kitchen, grunting like a caveman. He tossed her on the bed, yanked his and her clothes off, and fell on her, kissing, grasping, touching, stroking, and trying like hell to get his fill as if it were the last chance he had.

"Whoa, baby, slow down," she said at one point, until he grinned and dropped between her legs, using his lips and tongue to remind her that there was no reason to slow down.

Once she'd sung high opera with her climax, he licked his way up her torso, hitting both lush, hard nipples, then nibbling her neck until he found her mouth.

"Okay, you don't have to slow down now." And together they rocked in unison until the room filled with their mutual cries of satisfaction.

"I love you, Sophie," he said, remaining connected with her. "I want you to be with me forever."

She stared hard at him, as if trying to sort out a puzzle, then kissed him lightly. "I know. I love you, too. But...."

He sighed and rolled off her, resigned to wait it out as long as necessary. He'd said his piece. No more hiding for him. He knew what he wanted. She just had to admit it, too.

Chapter Eighteen

Sophie watched him as he ate, amused and pleased by his boyish energy at the task. Her gut was too topsy-turvy to even consider consuming food. How in god's name had she landed here with this incredible man? A near perfect combination of strong and weak, of commanding and vulnerable, who'd grown into a mature self-awareness after a few months with her.

She sipped water, willing her face not to reveal her news. She still didn't know how to process it. But she'd been living with it for almost three weeks and figured she could keep it to herself a while longer.

God, Soph, you're being so lame. Just like those damn secret baby romance books your mom used to devour weekly. You owe him the truth, especially about this.

But she ignored the inner nag, happy to be with him, relaxed and enjoying a meal. They chatted about the team. She filled him in on the news that Frank had been sent to jail to await trial, unable to make the bail the judge set, thank god. All the while, the Huge Unspoken Elephant in the Room sat on her chest, making it hard to breathe.

She touched his arm as he sipped water and scanned the Internet for soccer news. "How are you guys handling your injury?"

He glanced at her. "I'm playing. You know that. What else is there to handle?"

"It's not safe, Robert." She got to her feet and walked over to him, straddling his lap, loving the warmth of his torso against hers. "You know that."

Kissing his forehead, running her palms across his broad shoulders, she lifted his shirt, relishing the landscape of him. Amazed all over again that she had this amazing man right under her. "Please. Don't take the chance." She tried to pour all she had into the plea. To make him grasp how important it was, now, especially.

Tell him. He deserves to know.

He grasped her hips and stared straight into her soul. Her Brody. Her savior. Her project. Her man. "You don't understand. It's...." He looked up at the ceiling. But her ire rose, unstoppable, like an onrushing wind, filling her ears with noise even as he spoke. "I spent too many years of my life preparing for this. I'm not gonna throw it aside because I got bonked on the back of the head. I'm fine," he insisted, running large, warm hands up her arms, to her neck and into her hair. He shot her a wicked grin at the distinct movement under his shorts beneath her. "I'm more than fine. C'mon, I'll show you."

Holding him close, and with her body on high alert, she kept the threatening tears at bay. He moved her shorts aside and again they were connected. Groaning low in his throat, he sucked her nipples and he brought her body to a pulsing climax.

"Brody," she whispered. "I have to tell you something." She dug her fingers into his bare shoulders, into the ink covering his biceps.

"Mmmm hmmm...," he muttered into her breasts. "Okay. Tell me."

She rose up slightly, then lowered down onto him, staring into his eyes, loving him more than she had ever imagined loving another human in her life. The chair moved across the kitchen floor as she changed her angle, wanting him deeper. The second orgasm surprised her, blinding her. He grunted and tensed beneath her, his heat inside and out, making her want to weep with pleasure and now, fear.

This is not the time.

Not until she sorted out how she felt about it.

He clutched her, his breathing calming. "You never told me...." Lifting his lips to hers, he kissed her, dizzying her.. "What is it, Sophie Lynn? My love," he whispered into her neck.

"Nothing." She released him and stood up. Re-fastening her robe, she cradled his rough cheek, memorizing his face. "I've got ice cream."

He smacked her ass as she walked away. "That's my girl," he said, grabbing his tablet computer again.

• • • •

BRODY PLAYED THREE games without incident. She watched from her perch in the executive suite, sipping ginger ale and glad-handing investors and fat cat corporate box owners. Trying not to hyperventilate every time a fast break headed toward his goal.

Some smart ass with a phone had recently snagged a photo of them together at a nondescript Ann Arbor dive bar, kissing in a pretty obvious way which had made its way into the public eye. So they'd been outed. Now officially a G in the WAGs brigade, she didn't mind as much as she thought she might. She had other, bigger issues to consider. She'd even gone to a public event with him where there had been plenty of photos of them all dressed up and together as an Official Couple.

He'd stayed alone at his condo during this long stretch of back-to-back matches, and she respected his space. But by this point, at the fourth game in six days on their home field, her loneliness and pent-up sexual energy were making her crazy.

She gnawed the inside of her cheek, watching the clock, willing it to hurry the fuck up and be over so he would be safe. The match had been a near blow-out for the Black Jacks, 4-0 at the seventieth minute. The teams were jostling a lot though, which worried her. She made small talk with some big shot auto guys, sipping, and trying not to stress out.

Ten weeks, Sophie, the doctor had said. You have to make the call soon.

She closed her eyes. She had zero pregnancy symptoms. No nausea, no dizziness or tiredness. Horny as hell, but that should be expected, considering she hadn't been around her man for over a week. She didn't even want to admit the truth to herself, and spent hours each day in big-time denial. What did it matter? The fact remained that she, a woman in her early forties, had no business whatsoever having a kid...his kid.

Yeah, sure, but you "forgot" to get your quarterly birth control shot, didn't you, you craven liar.

Chancing a glance out onto the field, she touched the glass separating them from the public at the sight of a fast break headed at full speed toward him. "Move. You idiot," she whispered. "Oh, Brody, please." She leaned in, willing the stubborn man to get the hell out of the way.

The resulting, epic collision inside goal got replayed over and over on every sports channel for a while, until someone in her department contacted someone else and it stopped being shown. Arms, cleated feet, knees, skulls collided. She couldn't even tell who hit whom, and who went down. Until they all got up, including Brody. Blowing out a breath, she turned. Jack was there, smiling at her.

"He's fine, see?" He pointed as the object of their mutual interest kicked the ball he'd saved almost all the way into the opposing goal. "Nice pick, sister."

"Go to hell, Gordon," she said, but couldn't resist a huge grin.

She waited for Brody afterward, standing outside her car, fiddling with her phone, re-reading emails to try to quell rising anxiety. The third woman she'd interviewed to be the new, improved, and non-pregnant Madame Katrina seemed promising. She had a trial run that night with a new client. Dante sent her encouraging updates via text. Brody snuck up on her as she paced around, texting with her business partner.

"Put the phone away. I require your undivided attention." His low voice sent a shiver down her spine. "Goddamn, I am horny," he said, burying his nose in her neck. The words, ten weeks, rolled around in her brain.

"Okay, I can accommodate the superstar goalie, I suppose."

He gripped her ass, pressing an unmistakable erection into her hip, and she felt a strange urge to giggle. "Feels like a play night to me," she said, almost breathless with anticipation.

"Yep. It is." Opening her door, he helped her in and got behind the wheel. He sat for a minute, staring out the windshield. Busy putting her phone in her purse and buckling her seatbelt, Sophie finally figured out he hadn't moved for several seconds.

"You okay?" She put a hand on his arm, a small lick of panic tickling her nerves.

He shook his head, seemed to snap out of his trance, then blinked at her. "Sorry." he said, wiping his face. "Zoned out a second. I'm all about getting home now. Your place or mine?"

She leaned into him and put her palm on his zipper. "Your call, but I'm guessing the closer, the better." She kissed his neck. "I have something to tell you."

"Condo it is," he claimed, still grinning. Her heart turned over, realizing this was her moment, when she finally owned her happiness.

He drove in silence. When they pulled into his underground parking, she sensed something had gone horribly wrong. He parked and stared into the middle distance in silence. "Brody." She shook him. "Honey. What is it?"

His smile looked strange as he stumbled around to her side of the car. She got out and grabbed onto his arm.

"Goddamn it, Robert. Talk to me. Do you know where you are? What day is it? What's your full name?" The concussion test questions fell from her lips, and he answered them correctly.

They got in the elevator, hit his number, and she stared in horror as both his pupils dilated at once. He put his fingers to the bridge of his nose. Her heart pounded as the lift rose, and she smacked the first floor button again, determined to get him back in the car and to the hospital.

The doors opened, but he remained still, hanging onto the railing, his eyes wild and full of fear. "Sophie," he whispered, before he slid to the floor.

••••

THE ROOM SWAM INTO view. Images crisscrossed his brain. Soccer balls. Teammates. Strange homes. Indifferent, drunk parents. Lonely nights spent scrounging for Campbell's soup dinners and doing homework alone. A set of handcuffs, and with it, pain so exquisite, he grunted and sat up.

He struggled to stay seated, woozy and sick, weak in body and mind. Where in god's name was he? Dear Christ, had he blown his knee out? He touched them both, reassured by the lack of bulkiness under the covers.

"Thank god," he muttered. He had to be able to play. All he could ever count on boiled down to one word—soccer. The field, the pitch, was the one place he was happy, needed, counted on, loved even, by various sets of coaches and teammates for his fierce dedication to the sport.

His fingers met thick bandages when he touched them to his forehead. Why did his damn head feel like it weighed a thousand pounds? Groaning, he hit the nurse button. Where was everybody? He called out, or tried to, but his cracked, dry lips didn't want to cooperate.

"Hey! Can I get some water?" he croaked, but it came out sounding drunk. His tongue filled his mouth like a cotton ball.

A slow, rolling anger gained ground in his brain. It was a fury and frustration the likes of which he had never experienced. His skin was hot, and his eyes burned. Both of his hands were curled into tight fists. Shaking, he shifted his legs to the side of the bed. The dark room pissed him off. The lack of human response made it worse.

Goddamn, his head hurt. The room fuzzed out when he attempted to get up, but he muscled through it, channeling the near-fever pitch fury to fuel him. "Where the fuck is everybody?" He walked slowly to the door, but the transition from pitch-dark room to brightly lit hospital hall sliced through his skull like an acid-coated steel blade. Staggering back, he grabbed onto something and managed to pull the IV pole off the bed on his way to the floor.

Disembodied faces appeared, confusing him, and pissing him off more.

"It's like I suspected." The man who spoke grunted when Brody's foot connected with his groin.

"Get off me," he growled. "Get me out of here. Fuck!" He gasped when someone gripped his shoulders and pinned him to the hospital floor like a bug. He thrashed, lashing out, connecting with soft body parts and hard tile. But the sensation of operating someone else's body, like a marionette, all the while standing to the side, watching, waiting for something, or someone, to appear, made him want to puke.

"Calm down," a deep voice said. He glared at the dark face of a total stranger dressed in some kind of black and red soccer warm-up gear.

"Fuck you," he barked, jerking his arms, trying to reach the needle they had jammed into his arm. A nurse fumbled around, trying to keep his hands still.

"Hold onto his wrist, Rafe," the dark-faced guy said. Another man with similar features clamped down on the arm not punctured and currently bleeding from where he'd half-successfully ripped out the IV.

"Who are you?" he rasped, his throat dry and sore. "Help me get out of here. I have a game. We... we're in the playoffs... or... something. Ow. Ow!" he cried when the room blazed with the light of the sun directly into his brain. "Oh, Christ." Nausea surged up his gut.

"Watch out!" The nurse shoved her way through the crowd of men it took to hold him still, pulled him upright, and shoved a plastic tub under his mouth. He dry-heaved, his ribs aching and head pounding, shivering all over, unable to stop. He sat on the floor, drooling and staring at the room full of strangers who stared back at him while terror blanketed his nerves. Rage ripped through his chest once more, but he took a breath, trying to be calm.

The door flew open, revealing a woman dressed in jeans and a turtleneck. He noticed her attractive curves, long brown hair, and huge blue eyes streaming with tears. What had he done to make her cry? He hated it when women cried. Went out of his way to avoid it at all costs. She knelt beside him. Her perfume and other random scents filled his head, swirling around as if trying to find a resting place, or a familiar space, then wafted out, leaving him bereft and more confused than ever.

A name flashed across his brain. "Kelli?" he said, weakly. "Is that you?" He attempted to fake his way out of the fact that he lay here, surrounded by people, including a crying woman. And he had no fucking idea who any of them were.

Part Two
Chapter One

• • • •

THREE YEARS LATER

Sophie leaned back and stretched her legs out under the desk. It had been a brutally long day by any workaholic standards, beginning with having to bail out one player after a rowdy hotel party got busted by the cops. Now, nearly nine hours into contract negotiations and arm wrestling liability insurance companies after an alarming rate increase, she wanted to crawl into a bed and sleep for days.

In the three years since that horrible moment sitting on the hospital floor with the man she loved who no longer knew her name, she'd traveled a long road. She picked up the photo in the handmade, crooked frame studded with giant sloppy hearts and glued on doodads. The small, earnest face peered back at her, giant dark eyes shining with delight, thick black hair messy and windblown. She touched the image of the one person on the entire planet who truly mattered to her. The little boy whose very existence reminded her that she had purpose, could be the single parent, and that she owed it to him to be the best possible human and mature adult.

She sighed, shrugged off the late afternoon sinking spell in anticipation of seeing her son who never failed to make her simultaneously happy and exhausted. A sharp rap at the door startled her. When she glanced up, the carbon copy of the boy, writ large as a man filled the doorway, smiling crookedly. A shiver shot down her spine. Replacing the picture on her desk, she got to her feet.

"So, Brody." She picked up a piece of paper. "I'm entertaining some interesting requests from your..." She stopped, throat closing in jealous, useless anger. "Agent."

He sauntered in, his body firm and lean in the suit the players donned after every match. His loose-limbed comfort in his own skin made her want to scream, throw things, and launch into his arms.

Oh hell no, tried that, remember? And how well that ended for you?

She took time to blink, reminded her lungs to operate properly, but didn't let on he had affected her in any way, shape, or form.

"Yeah." He chuckled, running a hand through his still-damp hair. She gulped with the memory of that gesture. It was so quintessentially Brody-is-nervous, it sent a shaft of real pain through her gut. "Amber is a little...."

"She's being a pushy cunt, and you can tell her I said that." Sophie slammed the paper down on her desk and glared at him. "I'm sick of her trying to weasel you out of your contract with us. We're not ready to let you go. No matter how high your own opinion is of yourself."

Leveling her gaze at him, she marveled at how unbelievably handsome he was, sitting there, arm draped over the back of the chair, one leg crossed, ankle to knee. "You aren't worth that much. Not yet. So tell your agent-slash-girlfriend to back off." She willed back the stupid tears. Once she had herself under control, she glared at his smirk. "You can go now."

She turned to her laptop, pretending to ignore him, but his still-familiar scent filled her nose, her head, that subtle, clean-smelling cologne barely covering the near ground-in odors of leather, grass, turf, and sweat.

God, I miss him so much.

"You deaf?" she asked, not looking at him, willing him to leave.

"Damn, you're hot when you're pissed." His slow, smooth drawl settled deep in her gut.

She frowned. "Go away."

"If you insist, but I still remember our little moment in here." He rose, slowly, unfolding his body a little at a time, as if teasing her. Luckily, it only served to piss her off even more.

"I don't," she lied through her teeth. Because she remembered every blessed second of it. He chuckled again, and she said, "Beat it. I have grown-up things to do."

The odd, flat expression on his face, as if she'd struck him, gave her pause. It almost seemed as if he were remembering something. Her heart sank to her feet. She quite literally felt it sliding down her ribcage as the onslaught of memory struck her hard. She used to say that to him, as a joke, when he'd tease her back to bed on a Sunday morning or when he'd send blatantly sexy texts during the middle of her workday before his practice started. They stood, frozen, as if facing off in some kind of duel, as the memory of their last encounter in this room swirled through her psyche.

• • • •

"BRODY," SHE SAID, DESPERATE to make him remember, to force whatever part of his brain that had closed off everything to him before the surgery, to see her and recall what they had. "Come in." She watched his eyes as she shut the office door. Her early resolve to Madame-Katrina him into a subspace so his poor, shattered mind would open up and receive the memories that were no doubt beating against his skull, had slipped. She didn't want to dominate him. She wanted him to remember her.

"Um, sorry, I'm a little...." He pulled at his sweaty practice shirt, ran his fingers through his hair. "But coach said you needed me... um... it's urgent that I get up here. I hope I'm not in trouble, seeing as how you're the legal lady and all." He blatantly stared at her from head to toe in a way that might make her tingly, if it wasn't so out of character for him. That man—her Robert, as she thought of him—would never be so crass. They'd had a lot of laughs over his innate, Southern gentlemanly ways.

"Yes, well." She kept her distance, suddenly unsure about this being a good idea, no matter how hard her body clamored to leap across the divide and snatch his clothes off. "I thought we should talk."

The man who faced her now in her office was an all-new Brody, without a shred of doubt. He cocked a hip and an eyebrow. The room seemed to spin around her. What the hell? She had control in this goddamn room. Clearing her throat, she attempted to shake the oncoming white noise, signaling a mental place she hadn't inhabited for years.

"Why do you really want me here, Sophie, isn't it?" he asked, moving closer, like a dancer, fluid, graceful, hypnotizing her.

She shook her head and maintained her vigil at the door. "No, I mean, yes, but it's not...." He was too close, too perfect, and her desperation at a fever pitch. She let it happen, wrapping around him, kissing him, yanking his shirt up and off, his shorts down, eager and terrified in equal measure to get him back, the real Brody, her Brody.

"Oh, yeah," he growled, gripping her ass and plopping her up on her desk. His hand slid up her skirt. Fingers that were familiar and strange, soft and rough, eager and hesitant, made their way into her panties, stroked her, teased her, and forced a cry from her throat that surprised her.

"Hmm, nice." He grinned. "Let's have some more of those, shall we?"

She wanted to claw at him and drag her Robert out and into the light of day. But when he leaned in to kiss her, his gaze softened, became so breathtakingly familiar she very nearly blurted out he, Mr. Soap Opera Level Amnesia, would soon be a father.

"Oh," she said instead. And with one slow, firm stroke of his hips he filled her and they moved as one, lips locked and sweat mingling. It was ugly, fast, and the most satisfying physical act she'd had in weeks.

"Yes!" she yelped when he thrust deep and bit down on her shoulder.

He shuddered, groaned, and came with a rush of energy that did make her cry. Was he back? His dark-inked chest and shoulders, his very scent sharpened as they caught their breath. The face she clutched between her palms looked satisfied and smug, which shattered her fragile hope like a precious holiday ornament hitting a hardwood floor.

"Wow, legal lady." He shivered, pulling out of her. "A guy could get used to that kind of conference." With a grin, he yanked up his shorts. She stood, biting her lip, on the cusp of the sort of confession that changes lives forever. "Call me anytime you need more meetings." He patted her ass.

She yanked her skirt down, whirled on him, words burbling to the surface. "Well, enjoy the first and last time you get that sort of meeting from me," she ground out. "You don't deserve me, Brody Vaughn. Anything about me." She put a protective hand on her stomach, which had lately become noticeably fuller, at least to her eyes. "Go to hell. Don't come back."

She turned before the hurt on his face weakened her. Not her Robert J. Vaughn anymore and likely never would be. He was Brody, newly minted, king man-whore, in a land of men just like him.

"Fucking soccer players," she muttered, wiping away tears. She wouldn't cry over him anymore. Fate, or karma, or some bitchy combination of the two had reality-slapped her. She got it now. "Go," she whispered.

"Sophie," he said, his voice rough, cracked.

She risked a glance at him, and saw the face of a broken boy, unloved, and unable to love, the one she'd rescued from himself while he did the same for her. Gasping, she took a step forward. But he stumbled back, pulled the door open, and ran out.

Within a week, she'd called a meeting with all the coaches, team captains, and Jack in attendance. Every single one of them had been told not to tell Brody about the meeting. She hoped they believed she had that power because she wasn't sure she did.

They assembled, crammed into her office, in various states of sleepy and pissed off at six in the morning. She marched in, shut the door, and perched on the edge of her desk, mustering every ounce of pure bitch energy she had left. It had worked for her once. It would have to work now. She willed it so.

"All right Sophie, we're here. What is it?" Metin's soft voice and worried scrunched-up expression almost forced a hysterical laugh to burst from her mouth.

She put a hand to her lips to hold it back, took a breath, and pointedly met every last set of eyes in the room.

"I am pregnant," she stated. Jack exchanged glances with Rafe. The group took it in without comment or movement. She cleared her throat, unwilling to lose it like a typical girl in this room of man-boys. "You all know that Brody and I were together. Before that final crisis, because we let him continue to play injured." She pinned Nicco Garza with a pointed look that he had the graciousness to blink away from, his face red. "We were together," she said again. "I know you all know that, and so as you might expect, this is his child I'm carrying. But here is what you now know about it going forward" "

Standing, she pointed at each of them, ending with Jack. "As far as you are concerned, this is a goddamned immaculate conception, a real Virgin Mary kinda deal, get me? Because if I hear that he knows that it's his kid, I will come after each and every one of you with a castration knife first, clutching a legal document declaring you unfit to play or coach ever again." She glanced at Jack, her breathing ragged. He shook his head, as if to say, don't worry about me blabbing.

She sucked in a breath and at that moment began what amounted to an entirely new chapter of the Sophie Lynn Harrison Fucked-Up Book of Life. "I will be a mother to his child. But he'll never know it's his. Never. Now get the hell out. I have work to do."

The room seemed stunned into quiet, then Jack rose. "You heard her, boys. Move along." He waited as the room emptied. Turning to her, he said, "Sophie, listen...."

But she stopped him. "Nope. No words necessary. It's not rocket science, being pregnant and having a kid. I've got this. It will be fine." Dropping into her seat, she tried not to scream. She had no one, really. Her parents were long gone. She had no close girlfriends to speak of. She had Dante, of course, and his boyfriend.

And she had herself. As always. Which had worked thus far. Why would it stop working now?

Jack touched her shoulder, but she didn't move. Finally he left, shutting the door with a firm click.

• • • •

NOW, HERE SHE WAS, full-circle three years later, staring down the business end of Brody's dark gaze, which seemed full of remorse. She clenched her jaw and crossed her arms over her chest. Finally, he left, trailing the last vestiges of anything like reconciliation.

What's left to reconcile, anyway? He's not the man you met and fell head over heels with, like some stupid weakling. Get over it. You have a new purpose now, and you damn well know it.

She picked up the picture again, held it to her chest, and tried not to cry.

Chapter Two

Brody observed the show in front of him as he put a glass of something that smelled strong and tasted stronger to his lips. A man walked onto a small stage, sporting nothing but a giant, straining erection and a smile at the sight of two equally naked hot chicks on the bed. They'd been busy for about the last half hour, between acrobatic sixty-nines, loud moaning.

Brody touched his crotch, acknowledging his own arousal. Who wouldn't be turned on? It was expected of him. He glanced around at the other people observing the live sex show at the party he'd been invited to, along with his agent-girlfriend who, at the moment, was part of the show as one of the chicks on the bed.

Funny how that fact didn't bother him in the slightest. He felt a little clinical about it actually, as if he were watching himself, watching his girlfriend get eaten out by a girl.

Nicely done, he thought at one point. Have to remember that move next time I go down on her.

Sipping the alcohol, he wished it had the desired effect. The man let the girls pull him onto the huge bed. Brody leaned forward, his cock painfully trapped behind his zipper. He was horned up, but also somehow numb. That's how he rolled—and he liked it. He stood, got closer, so he had a better view as the man flipped his agent/girlfriend over onto all fours and slid his huge dick into her.

Brody loved that part, the penetration moment, the actual physical connection. His pulse raced, while the rest of him prepared to get in on the action. The other girl kissed the strange man while he pounded into Brody's girlfriend from behind.

He stripped out of his jeans, breathing a sigh of relief as he dropped onto the bed, groaning when the other girl pounced on him and swallowed his cock nearly to the base, before moving up and down his shaft, poking her tongue into the slit, licking around the head.

The word nice kept floating through his head—better than nice. He turned to see his agent/girlfriend make her O-face, saw her tits jiggle with every pound from behind. Putting his arms behind his head, he played audience, observing as she came with that funny detached feeling again, no longer even sensing the girl's lips or tongue while she still sucked on him like a lollipop.

"Okay, stop." He pushed her off him in disgust.

Amber dropped down beside him and ran her fingertips over his chest. She tweaked his nipples hard, bit his shoulder, and palmed his slowly-softening shaft. "Poor baby," she whispered. "Numb again?"

He nodded, agitated, antsy, wanting to get the hell out of there, but needing to stay, needing something...someone...not here and not these people.

Somebody put a flogger in Amber's outstretched palm. Grinning, she gave it to him and his body revved up again, ragingly painful erection and all.

"Give it to her," Amber whispered in his ear, her arms draped around his neck from behind. She pointed to the girl who knelt at the foot of the bed, her eyes cast down. "She wants you to. Show me, Brody." She pinched both his nipples so hard he groaned.

Getting to his feet, he pointed to the bed without a word. The nameless, naked girl bent over it, and he smacked the sweet flesh of her ass until she moaned and writhed. He smelled her ripe, raw, lusty desire.

"Fuck her, Brody," Amber yelled from her new position in front of him, fingers already down between her own legs again. Another naked girl had fallen into their mix. She went down on Amber—Jesus, am I dating a lesbian?—and he blinked. He'd never known a girl who liked getting head as much as Amber did.

He dropped the flogger and pounded into the girl, again and again, letting the orgasm take control, continuing to smack her hips and ass. Finally, she gripped his cock hard, cried out, and pulled him right over the edge. His hips bucked, he released his load into her then pulled out nearly immediately, done with this scene, over it, sick of it and with himself.

....

BRODY'S SKIN TINGLED and his spine relaxed under the hot shower in a way he only got after a monster orgasm. His head had that odd, annoying, echoing feeling he'd been experiencing more and more lately. The scalding hot water hit his face. He pressed his thumbs to his eyes. The parade of images had begun again, and he was powerless against them. He groaned and propped his hands on the tiled wall, but the memories invaded despite his willing them away.

A large woman with a cigarette dangling from her mouth laughed at him, a throaty, raspy noise that made his heart beat fast with anxiety. She pointed at him, while a fat, sloppy-looking boy stood at her shoulder, smirking. Shame flooded his nerve endings that he had no reason to feel. His knees shook. He slid down the wall, helpless against the onslaught.

The next one showed up right on cue, like it had pretty much every night for the last two weeks or so. A girl, a pretty one, stared right at him. She wore a long, formal gown and tugged at him until they were in a dark room, fumbling around, kissing like the amateurs they were. His dick hardened under the shower water. The sensation of impending disaster crept into his brain, lodged there, at the memory of kissing the girl's lips, groping her small, exposed breasts, and then, a telltale tingling in his spine and....

"Oh...unh...." He grunted, and her face fell. She gathered up her dress and flounced out, leaving him a smelly mess, the trousers he hadn't even taken off dark in the crotch from his spunk.

"Jesus." Brody gave up and flopped to his butt, while the images bombarded him, reminders of moments he would swear happened to someone else but were inexorable in their ramp-up. Every day he got a new one to add to the rest. His heart pounded, chest tightened with anxiety when a drop-dead sexy woman appeared at the front of what appeared to be a classroom. She had long red hair piled up on her head. Her curves were emphasized by the clingy dress and heels she wore, but made teacher-appropriate somehow by the square glasses she peered through.

He shoved that image away, his whole body convulsing with the effort. "Fucking leave me alone!" he shouted into the empty shower room. "Fucking bitch!" He scrambled to his feet, got out, and dried off.

Fury blinded him. The sort of anger dangerous to anyone nearby crowded every corner of his aching skull. The fits of poisonous and painful rage hit him more and more lately. Sucking in a deep breath and counting to ten, twenty, then fifty helped a little. At least he managed to get dressed. Requiring fresh air, he barreled through the sex room, heading for the door.

Confusion, hurt, anger, fear, and a small lick of dread rolled around in a sick, breathless stew. He walked out and started for his motorcycle. God, he loved that thing. A long ride would clear his head.

"Brody!" A female voice hit his ear. He turned, not recognizing her for a second. Then sighed.

"Oh, uh, hey, Amber. I gotta go. Can you get a ride...home?" He gulped. She actually lived with him now, he realized with a sinking feeling.

"I guess. You okay, baby doll?" she asked, starting toward him across the giant lawn of the house where they went to fuck other people, and sometimes each other while other people got off watching them.

He winced when another image hit his poor, ragged brain. Another woman. Her—the legal lady, with her long brown hair, huge blue eyes, her determined face...and that ass...he clenched his fists and glared at Amber.

"No. I'm not, but I will be after a long ride," he said, gripping his keys and praying she didn't come any closer.

She drew a large robe around her thin frame. "All right," she said. "Hey, did you talk to the BJ's owner yet?"

"Not now, Amber. I need some space. See you later, I guess. At home."

Sophie's words flashed through him: pushy cunt...and no matter how high your opinion of yourself...we aren't ready to let you go.

Thing was, he didn't want to leave the BJs as they'd started referring to themselves. The Black Jacks were the only thing resembling consistency and family that he had now. He knew full well that Amber, his agent/girlfriend/swinger pal, had determined to get him away from them for some reason. To line her own pockets he figured, but she must have another motive. He'd picked up on her time to settle down together and not in this shithole called Detroit vibe one too many times already.

He shook his head, climbed on the bike, and smiled at the throaty rumble vibration underneath him. His heartbeat slowed. His head stopped aching. And he rode, finally finding a small bit of peace.

Chapter Three

Sophie juggled the grocery bags, her laptop case, and a giant bag of cat food into the house, barely making it to the kitchen counter before dropping everything all over the floor. Sighing, she stared at the jumble of bags, owning up to how exhausted she'd been these last few days. Player trade season sucked every year, but this year had been especially awful, given that several of their key players, including Brody, were being heavily courted away by bigger, more famous teams.

She had the food tucked into the pantry and fridge within a few minutes and a chicken casserole into the oven a half hour later. Glancing at the clock, she acknowledged she'd been measuring her life in ten and twenty-minute increments for almost three years, and that it seemed, to her anyway, part and parcel of motherhood.

Ten more minutes of sleep while the newborn snuffled around, pre-waking and demanding food. Twenty stolen while napping together before having to get up to do some work. And yet ten more over coffee, before the rambunctious boy rose for the day, feet hitting the floor at a dead run. Of course, the twenty before he got home from his afternoon play date, driven there by the young girl who cared for him during the day, allowing Sophie a single glass of wine while dinner bubbled away in the oven. She caught her reflection in the dining-room window. She, Sophie Harrison, had a nurturing gene that included breastfeeding and gazing at her baby's face for hours on end. And now, making healthy meals every night? Shocking.

"Mommy!" The voice shattered the illusion of peace, bringing the chaos of her life back into focus. "Mommy! Mommy! Mommy! Mommy!"

Sam always greeted her that way, like a worried puppy, convinced it must be dumb luck that he got to see her again, as if she would disappear forever unless he acted ecstatic at every greeting. Incredible, really, the sheer power of her child's love for her. Not to mention as intimidating as hell. Every day he amazed her all over again, terrifying her and charming her by his existence.

She welcomed the full force of his strong little body into her arms. He always grabbed on for dear life for a few minutes, his sweet-smelling face tucked into her neck until she peeled him off, usually so she could move on to whatever next step their busy life held. Sometimes, she honestly believed he would stay wrapped around her if she'd let him.

The progression of obsession with her child could be measured not only in ten-minute increments but also by how he felt in her arms. The terrifying, small, helpless like a baby bird newborn. The six-month-old baby who would draw stares from strangers everywhere they went. Everyone always wanted to touch his chubby, angelic face in the grocery store and at the park or the pool, which made her want to smack their grubby hands away from him.

The early toddler, a full-on walker by ten months, running by a year, steady and energetic. Now a child on the verge of actual little-boyhood who currently held her so tight she had a hard time breathing. She smiled at his sitter and disentangled his arms from her neck, hating to do it because soon enough she'd be begging him for hugs.

Funny how the super-independent, former law firm partner, in-control Dominatrix, attorney for one of the most popular new pro sports teams in the region might be reduced to near tears by the feel of her son's arms around her.

"Hey, Sam. How was the park?"

"Hot," he declared, frowning down at his eternally dirty fingernails. "Mommy." He put both hands on her cheeks, preparing to impart one of his classic Serious Sam Observations. "Some dogs were being funny. I saw them. I thought they were dancing. Jen told me they were doing some mommy-daddy things." His sober gaze never flinched or appeared amused in any way. She had a hard time keeping the laughter from escaping her lips.

Jen set his backpack and water bottle on the table and grabbed her purse. The twenty-one-year-old college student on the outs with her parents and taking some time off from classes to find herself, represented savior-hood for Sophie. She'd found her through a friend, and her references as babysitter had been impeccable, so she'd become a crucial part of the family.

"Sorry," she mouthed behind Sam's back, miming with her fingers what the dogs had actually been doing.

"Okay then," Sophie said, wanting to set Sam down so she could pay Jen for the week. The boy kept his grip on her face, his eyes narrowing. She sat still, waiting for him to finish his thought.

"Where is my daddy?" he asked, surprising her. This had never come up before, no matter how many other kids' daddies crossed his path.

She wracked her brain, unwilling and unready for that particular conversation.

"I told you, Samster," Jen said, tugging him off his mother's lap and swinging him around in a circle, one of his favorite pastimes. "Your daddy just figured your mommy could handle things on her own, and you guys didn't need him around."

The boy's delighted squeals hurt Sophie's ears. She realized that this wouldn't be the last of the lack-of-father related questions. Sam would fixate on it, worry it like a dog with a bone, and come back to her demanding more. But for now, she went with the babysitter's view. All she required, the one perfect thing left to her now, was the small boy with dark hair and a smile that lit up any room he entered.

• • • •

AFTER DINNER, BATH, an hour of Lego wars and a puzzle, Sam nestled into her side while she read his favorite book, Love you Forever, with its tales of toddler, childhood, and teenager woes and then the aging mother, who for always and ever my baby you'll be. Able to recite the thing in her sleep, Sophie still let it get to her.

She listened to him breathe. Her son, Samuel Robert Harrison, the living, breathing, walking, running, talking perfect miniature of his father. He shifted, his ever-active mind not settling. The kid required little sleep and hadn't from the start. She had to use a routine to get him to wind down: warm dinner, thirty minutes of cartoons or a video, bubble bath with requisite singing, an hour of play—his choice—then a story or two.

"Mommy," he said, his voice sounding small and far away. "I'm sorry."

She kissed his hair, sucking in a huge breath of her son's clean-for-now little boy scent. "For what? You should never apologize for no reason, you know."

He sat up and pinned her with a dark stare. The compulsion to weep, to gnash her teeth, to call Brody, to make him come help her parent this beautiful, serious, scary child, held her in its brief, unreasonable grip. She shoved it away, as she'd been doing pretty much every day since Sam entered her world.

"I don't want a daddy. Daddies are dumb." A tear wobbled on the edge of his thick lashes.

"Oh, baby, no they're not. But in this house, it's you and me. We're the home team, okay?" She touched his nose, then hers, and he giggled, sniffled, and wiped the lone tear away.

"Like the Black Jacks?" He brightened, his newfound obsession with the real-life soccer players peopling his small world, forcing thoughts of absent daddies out of his head. Oh the irony, she thought for the millionth time.

She smiled and stood, covering him up with the blanket emblazoned with the logos of all the teams in the Black Jacks division, now that they'd been promoted out of expansion side status. His pillowcase and sheet had the ubiquitous black and red balls, his rug was as green as a soccer pitch, with the Black Jacks' logo in the middle. She sighed. Whoever said biology didn't count for much had shit for brains.

Granted, he'd been immersed in her life as lead attorney for a major league soccer team, had been in his baby seat during matches or when she worked in her office, players and coaches and marketing people coming and going, talking nothing but soccer.

"Yeah, Sam, like the Black Jacks."

The team dubbed him their official mascot, and he'd been allowed to watch and sometimes run alongside them as they prepared for practice. Nicco Garza in particular had warmed to him and for some reason, her son had taken to the normally surly, cynical, older player. Brody hardly gave Sam a second glance. He'd been so caught up in his own selfish world since the radical emergency surgery he'd undergone in a desperate attempt to relieve the pressure of his swelling brain, and that suited Sophie just fine.

Mostly.

She kissed both cheeks and his nose, their usual goodnight, and flipped off his lamp.

"Hey, Mommy," he said, his small voice nervous again.

Turning in the doorway, she tried not to let her irritation sound in her voice. She had another several hours' worth of work to do for her other job still. "What is it, baby?"

"When I laid on my bed after my bath, my penis stuck straight up in the air! And it kinda felt funny, like a tickle right on the end. So I touched it and it felt good but it kept standing straight up, even after I kept touching it."

"Oh," she said, her face heating up. "Well, that's normal." Making a mental note to consult her How to Raise a Boy to a Man and Not Lose Your Mind, or whatever title of the latest son-raising manual. "It's okay to touch it."

"I know. I was just telling you. G'night."

"Good night." She stumbled out of the room laughing until tears ran down her face. When the laughter became sobbing, she let it take her. Can't keep all that inside, after all. Then she poured a glass of wine and pulled out her laptop to read the latest reports from Dante—Katrina's was the name of her new company, a high-end, secret, and exclusive service for subs of all genders. She now employed men and women to provide whatever her clients wanted.

Between her and Dante, they'd cleared a million dollars profit the year before. She sipped and studied the numbers for the quarter, her tears drying. After a couple of hours of budgeting, working on schedules for the following two weeks based on the high demand for her employees' services, she rubbed her face and leaned back.

The purple-ish dusk deepened into full night, as it always did. A new day would dawn soon. Like usual.

Her life, the one she'd hastily constructed for herself and her son out of the ashes of yet another relationship disaster, advanced. She remained a tenant among homeowners on her quiet, tree-lined street, but she didn't care. The family-centric feel of the street suited her. But at quiet moments like this, memories of Brody came at her, incessant and relentless. She gave in to them and cried a bit more before crawling under the covers. No need to set a mechanical alarm because, despite the fact the next day was Saturday, her own little boy-shaped wake-up call would come at six a.m. without fail.

Chapter Four

"Harder! C'mon baby, fuck Amber like you mean it!"

Brody watched his cock, slick, wet, pounding in and out of the girl's body. He liked this moment, the almost money shot. It fueled a fresh surge of lusty adrenaline down his spine right when boredom threatened. Amber must have sensed it and ramped up the nasty talk on purpose. His fingers dug into the spare flesh of her hips.

"Spank Amber's ass, Brody. What are you waiting for? Act like a man! She's been very bad!" She whipped her head around, glared up at him as if he were failing.

That pissed him the fuck off. He observed, as if watching someone else, as his hand rose. He felt the stinging smack against his palm, again and again. He owned the brief moment of power it allowed him as Amber shrieked and arched her back, giving him an even deeper angle inside her.

He reached up and grabbed her hair, tugged, using it as reins, and rode her like a circus pony, no longer hearing her or feeling much of anything. The air whooshed over his vocal cords and his mouth opened wide. Blinded momentarily, he shivered, let go of her hair, and stepped away from her.

She'd declared his habit of disconnecting within seconds of orgasm as weird, but cute. He viewed it more like a necessity, a survival mechanism. He had to get away from her, from any woman he'd fucked, or the nearly overwhelming urge he always got to hold them close, kiss them, beg them like a little kid to never leave him alone. Because that sort of neediness made him feel strange.

He fought it by pulling his sometimes still-climaxing dick out of whatever pussy he'd been fucking, Amber's, or one of her accommodating friends, and standing still until that part of his anatomy finished.

He stumbled backward, suddenly dizzy. His hand stung. A sudden rush of shame punched an iron fist into his gut. "S-s-s-sorry," he stuttered, fascinated, as her still-visible sex continued to pulse, slick and wet, and at that moment the last thing he wanted to look at.

She sighed and flopped down on the bed onto her side, curling around a pillow. "Amber liked that, baby. Go get your shower. I know you want to."

He blinked. "Why do you do that?"

"Do what?" She rolled onto her back and stretched.

An absolute shark of an agent, she was savvy and possessed as cutthroat a business sense as any man in the industry. People both respected and feared her. He shook his head, recalling their first meeting when she'd picked him up at a bar, literally yanking him into a back hallway and blowing him like a pro while he stood there, palms pressed against the cold, concrete block wall.

It had been a turning point for him, and one he should likely thank her for initiating. Nearly a year's worth of hard partying, harder playing, winning games like a champ, and fucking every pussy in a twenty-mile radius had landed him at some nightclub, somewhere, damned if he remembered where. And Amber had appeared in his life, her green eyes shining, her barely there dress pulling his X-addled body like a magnet.

Now, sick of her and her manipulation, he had no idea how to cut her loose. He allowed this little truth—that his terror at what would happen to him if she did leave kept him from kicking her out of his life for good.

"Why do you talk about yourself as if you were someone else, you know." He cast around for the phrase, last heard in college Freshman English class. "Third-person-like."

She giggled and got up on all fours, her lips wet and inviting, her hair hanging down over her face. "What are you talking about? Now go get your shower, Brody. Or Amber is gonna jump that cock again,"

She glanced at the body part in question. So did he. His cock did indeed appear to still be jumpable. He touched it, pondering a second go-round. But with the realization that he couldn't feel his own palm on his most sensitive flesh and that his vision had gotten fuzzy around the edges in a now-familiar way, he scoffed and headed for the shower instead.

Amazing what the human brain would tolerate. He had become so completely detached from anything he did that didn't involve playing, practicing, or staying in shape for his sport, he thought he might be going legitimately insane. Shaking under the pounding streams of hot water, he warded off yet another onslaught of scary memories and panic. If he weren't pushing his body to its limits for soccer or fucking some girl, he had no control over what sort of freakish journey down mysterious memory lane his brain would take him.

Today's included yet more of the redhead, the teacher in the tight dress with the long hair, as if she stood right outside the shower door, dressed from head to toe in leather, including a mask. She had a whip in her hand. He flinched at its sting and bite. His cock stayed hard, loving the pain, but his brain headed into meltdown, begging her to stop, to let him be, to let him just hold her.

Then came a room, dark, but for a candle, a cross, cuffs, and pain all over. He had on nipple clamps and a cock ring, while she poured wax near his scrotum, teasing him, calling him names, telling him not to be such a baby, to man up and take it. Because she, his Mistress, had to get off—which was his only job.

Then, silence arose, as if the pain had spilled into another realm to be experienced by someone else. He stared unseeing at the tile wall as her face appeared—the woman with the red hair and leather. She straddled his hips, riding him, using him, coming again and again while pinching him hard to teach him how to deny his own natural release. And he had no pain, no pleasure. He just existed for her to use.

"Goddamn it!" He pounded the wall, willing her away from him. Her constant teasing did nothing but infuriate him for taking it for so long. Because she had dumped him like a prom date with herpes. He remembered it clear as day, now. It had dropped into his stupid brain like some kind of sick slide show in full color, full pain, full emotion.

He saw her when she looked up from her phone screen. Watched her gaze narrow as her wheels turned. "Go," she'd blurted out of the blue. He'd groveled, begged, sniveled like the baby she'd transformed him into, but she wouldn't listen because her job had been in jeopardy. So he had to go.

"Fuck you, bitch!" he yelled, loud, purging her. And she vanished into the gaping maw of his murky non-memory. He got out of the shower, dried off, and dressed. Amber sat in front of the TV in his robe. He glared at her. "I'm going to that club, downtown, The Suite. You can come if you want, but I need to try something. To see if it helps me remember."

"Oh, baby." She jumped up and wrapped herself around him, cooing in his ear, drawing him down onto the couch with her. "You do whatever you want to do. I've heard good things about that place. Kyle Summerlin, you know, the former NFL star, owns it." She pulled his head to her breasts, stroking his hair.

His cock stirred again as the evil, mysterious, red-headed, torturous female lurked around a corner, giggling and waiting for him to let his guard down. "Yeah," he muttered, staring into Amber's hard-angled face. She claimed to be helping him. But something told him he got the raw end of that deal. Growling, he flipped and had her pinned under him. He unzipped his jeans and shoved into her with a grunt, shutting out everything but raw physical sensation. So he could screw himself dry, raw, and empty of memory.

"Yeah, baby, that's more like it," she said.

After the second time around with Amber, he slept like the dead, but for a brief image of a different woman this time. Sophie Harrison, the legal lady he'd desk-fucked that one time and spent the next three days trying to get over the urge to go back to her again. And in his dream her blue eyes had no more anger, only deep relief.

Chapter Five

"I'm worried about Vaughn," Jack said, halfway through their usual Wednesday lunch and beer meeting.

She frowned over her glasses at him and kept quiet, hoping he'd get the message that the Robert J. Vaughn topic remained forbidden, outside of trade discussions that were heating up in a big way. Thanks in no small part to the hero he'd been in their latest season, diving and leaping and rolling and making the kinds of saves seen at the highest possible level of play. Well, that, and the grasping greediness of his agent, Amber London.

"Whatever," she said.

"He looks bad. He seems, I don't know, haunted or something. He's working out like a mad man, like he's obsessed. I'd worry about HGH if I didn't have them tested regularly." He sipped his beer.

She forced her heartbeat to calm. Brody's health or the possibility of doping didn't concern her. She had her own issues, plus a strange sort of date tonight, at a well-known BDSM club to do some clandestine investigation of how they ran their operations, and to scope out possible new employees. She'd lost one of her best men, his fiancée not keen on him continuing after marriage. And one of her very first female employees, a hot-as-shit, fifty-year-old woman, had decided to move to Europe. It was stressful as all get out. She had Katrina's booked well into the next quarter and couldn't afford to lose steam along the underground BDSM insider network by canceling appointments.

"Yo, earth to Sophie." Jack snapped his fingers under her nose. "He's not himself. I know that's stupid to say, considering that he's not, and hasn't been for a while now. But this new Brody seems to be slipping, like he's just off center, taking crazy chances in goal, getting directly in the line of fire on purpose. Like a death wish to go with his old head injury."

She sighed and finished her beer. "Jack, I'm sorry to hear that, but it's really not my concern." Her voice sounded way more confident about that fact than she felt.

"I know." Jack ran a hand around the back of his neck, blew out a breath, then picked up his weekly briefing sheet from her, resuming the discussion, leaving the delicate topic of Brody Vaughn behind.

• • • •

SHE GOT HOME EARLY on purpose, wanting to have some Sam time before she headed out for a late night. Jen had taken him to his afternoon playgroup and planned to hang around for dinner and sleep over.

"So you can, you know, have a real date." She waggled her eyebrows at Sophie, who blushed.

"Oh yeah, well. Maybe," she said, as casually as possible.

She and Sam had a game of tag out back, then he settled down with a puzzle, the only indoor activity that kept him still for longer than fifteen minutes. The cat they'd rescued from a shelter at Sam's insistence wound around his ankles, and he tugged the animal up onto his lap, clutching it while he studied the pieces in front of him.

So serious and focused, he thrilled and alarmed her both. She knew that he wouldn't get up from the table until the thing got done, but he'd mastered the pre-school puzzles in no time so she'd moved him up a level last week. Of course, if he didn't get it, he had been known to tip the coffee table over with a cry of frustration and stomp to his room, treating her to a door slam worth of any teenager.

She watched him, his brow furrowed as he moved the pieces around, studying them. After a few minutes, she walked into the kitchen and hit a preset number on her cell recalling that she wanted to do some research after Jack's comments earlier in the day.

"Hey woman. What's shaking?" The sound of her friend's voice on the phone brought a smile to her face.

"Hey, uh, I have another question about concussion and head trauma." Her voice shook at the end. She hated the sound of it. The other woman responded briskly, telling her what she wanted to know.

Sophie had had exactly five close female friends in her life, including this latest one, but she'd never been more grateful for her. She met Susan when she'd shown up at her obstetrician's office, distraught and crying, hopeless for her future with the man who'd gone under the knife one person, and awakened from surgery someone else—someone with no idea that he loved her. She demanded the abortion then, on the spot, would pay them as much as they wanted.

Susan, a nurse, had calmed her down, then held both her hands. "Tell me what happened," she'd said, in her soft, no nonsense voice.

And Sophie, always keen to guard her privacy, had spilled it, blurting out the whole stupid mess from start to finish. Susan handed her tissue after tissue, nodded her head at the right moments using appropriate sounds of shock and dismay at the right times during the stuttering narrative.

When she'd finished with that last horrible moment on the desk, when she'd let Brody fuck her like...like some kind of desperate cougar, Susan had stayed quiet. Finally she'd stood, crossed her arms over an ample chest, and said the oddest thing. "You sound like the sort of woman who would make a great mother to me."

Sophie had stared at her, shocked. "I'm not. I don't know anything about it. I mean. You don't even know me." She had touched the subtle bump under her shirt without thinking.

Susan had nodded, helped her to her feet, and guided her out with a sheet of prenatal instructions. By the time Sophie got home, still coming to terms with what she'd just copped to—that she wanted her baby so badly she already felt the warm bundle in her arms—she thought taking this crazy step might just be the thing that could transform her into the sort of person she'd always wanted to be.

Her phone had rung while she sat in the car that day, staring at her small house. It had been Susan, checking on her already. They'd been fast friends since, and Susan had actually been the one to deliver Sam thanks to his eagerness to meet the world, not giving her time to make it to the hospital. She'd been in labor without realizing it for half a day before heading to her regular weekly check-up with a heavy sensation in her lower half and twinges in her back.

"Congratulations, you're nearly fully dilated!" Susan had chirped, and within an hour Sam was in her arms thanks to the quick actions of her friend and the obstetrician who'd guided her through the pregnancy.

She'd picked Susan's brain over the concussion thing, too. Which helped her feel more in control of it. Brody had undergone severe head trauma and the surgery had saved his life but cost him his memory at the same time.

"The brain is the most mysterious organ in the universe," Susan had said once, over wine while Sam played with her young daughter, an adorable little girl with Down's Syndrome who Susan and her doctor-husband had adopted a year before Sam's birth. "Well, after the heart, that is. The one that makes us do stupid shit, not the one that pumps the blood."

Tonight, Sophie, pondered what her friend had said. As he got older, Brody would be susceptible to all sorts of maladies: seizure disorder, psychological breaks, muscle tremors, all sorts of nastiness. Even after he'd been told this, he'd jumped back into the goal, eager to return to his life, claiming if he were going to crap out eventually anyway, he would go down doing the one thing he loved.

The likelihood of his ever recovering all of his memory remained minimal. She wanted to help him. She'd given up on being anything to him other than the legal lady, however, and wouldn't reverse direction now.

After a quick shower, she checked her email again for the confirmation invite to The Suite, the most upscale, exclusive, destination BDSM clubs in the area. Frowning at Dante's latest missive, Hire More People!! as the subject line, she studied the tasteful, anonymous message she'd received when she clicked through their website to request to attend in a mask. She bit her fingernail, a flutter of doubt-filled second-guessing nearly forcing her to cancel the whole thing.

She had visited Kyle's club before, back when she was living a life that seemed so utterly removed from her current one, it was as if she, Sophie, were the amnesiac. Like Brody, in a strange limbo of the before and after for those around him, but for him, only the now.

She'd met Frank at Kyle's club. Once he'd laid claim to her after she'd forced Evan Adams out of her life for reasons that still remained mysterious to her, he had insisted they not attend anymore. Frank hadn't liked putting her out there for show, didn't like the club scene for them as a true D/s couple. Of course, he did it to control her. Ensuring that she stayed as isolated as possible had been the first step in his plan.

She glanced over at the large wooden box on her coffee table. Its dark mahogany wood, devoid of any decoration, meant more to her than any single item she owned or had ever owned in her life. Frank's secret stash, she'd learned, once he'd confessed under questioning before being slapped in jail for attempted murder and extortion, did exist. Right under her feet, as it were. He'd been squirreling away cash—her damn cash—and hiding it in plain sight.

It had been in the very box where he stored the sex toys, under a false bottom. The impressive collection of vibrators, dildos, and what not had concealed almost ninety-thousand dollars—the amount she'd paid back already to creditors through bankruptcy proceedings. So when it was revealed, the court awarded it to her.

Before she chickened out and let Frank and his memory force her from acting, she got up and headed for her bedroom. The few items of club-wear she still had were stuffed in the back of her closet. She dragged them out and prayed to the gods of lost baby weight she might still fit into them, before packing some into a leather bag. The manager of The Suite, Shannon, Kyle's fiancée, said she'd be allowed to change there. Jen had a bowl of popcorn and was watching TV when she emerged, heart pounding and face flushed with onrushing terror at facing that place again.

"Well, thanks again for staying over." She gripped the purse strap tight, hoping she didn't appear as wigged out as she felt.

"Sure thing." Jen smiled, then returned to whatever dreadful reality show blared from the television. "Have fun. I mean it."

"Oh, I'll try," she said, keeping it light and short as her heart played its terrifying rhythm against her ribs.

The pressure to hire more people, played havoc with her head as she drove the forty miles downtown, more or less on autopilot. The whole point of the night's undercover trip stayed fixed in her mind. She also wanted to refresh her memory as to how the club scene worked. It had been a long time since she'd darkened the door of such a place. With so much water under her personal bridge since then, the bridge might as well not exist.

Dante had been making noises about converting their private D/s service into something else. As of now, they had five rooms, each with its own theme and a fully booked calendar from now until the foreseeable future. He wanted to open it up some, so that the scheduling wouldn't be so nightmarish and the profit margins healthier. Not totally against that in concept, she wanted to check out how a top-shelf, perfectly run club did things from a customer's perspective. So, in the name of research and continued small business success, she headed straight back into her worst nightmare. That of potential submission to a total stranger. She was tingly with eagerness combined with a healthy dollop of anxiety.

• • • •

THE SUITE PROVED AS tasteful and lovely as she remembered. The memory rush, surprisingly, wasn't too negative. She'd had some amazing times there with Evan and a couple of mind-blowing sessions with Frank, on the rebound from her rejection of her onetime law firm intern.

She stared at herself in the mirror. The corset highlighted her pregnancy-improved boobs without a doubt. She was plenty comfortable in her new, mature body. Of course, that meant she had to ditch the leather pants and go with a garter belt, silk stockings, and lacy panties option but she doubted anyone would be complaining too much about that.

Damn, you are fine. She pep talked as she put her hair up, letting a few curly strands frame her face. Finally, she settled the mask over her eyes, adjusting the strap so it would be comfortable enough to leave on for a while, no matter what she ended up doing.

A soft knock at the door of her room signaled her primping hour over. It was show time. She sucked in a breath and followed Shannon out to the main room, forcing herself to recall the good memories and not let the ones of Frank ruin it for her. Because a new reality hit, then. She was big time, full-on, damp-panty, hard-nippled, near-panting, horny.

Her autonomous nervous system took over, and she shivered in pleasant anticipation. She might get laid, after a bit of playtime, BDSM-style, the likes of which she hated to admit that she missed.

These days, no one took security as seriously as Kyle. After the truth about Frank had finally emerged and shown that Kyle and his many layers of background checks and vetting had failed, letting a total faker into his club and into the life of one of his best customers, playing as a Dom at The Suite got harder than ever. She had registered under a pseudonym. Kyle honored her desire to remain anonymous, letting Shannon handle the direct contact using the name she'd provided without question. He trusted her motives, and she loved that about him. He likely knew that she wanted to scope out potential new Doms for her stable at the Katrina loft not that far from this one, but he didn't care. No one would replace The Suite as the premiere destination for the sort of kink they all enjoyed. And besides, Madam Katrina's was more of an a la cart experience, tailored, as it were, to the individual making the reservation for services.

Shannon led her onto the stage and Sophie forced her brain to shut down, keeping her gaze on the floor. She got to her knees when told to do so. Shoes appeared as the carefully chosen Doms presented themselves for her to consider. The usual drill, and one that bored her, gave her an inkling that the club scene might not be what she would do with Katrina's. Her mind had already begun formulating different strategies, pondering a suburban location as a way to alleviate stress on her calendar and accommodate all the needy folks who wanted to be whipped, spanked, caned, shackled, and humiliated by total strangers in leather.

A new set of shoes appeared and her neck moved of its own accord, earning her a swift yank of the chain attached to her collar. Her skin broke out in a cold sweat, then chills. Her nearly four-years-neglected body pulsed, throbbing as if already being touched by the man looming over her, kissed by his lips, and bound by his hands. A tear slipped from under the mask when the men moved back. She crawled on all fours in one direction, as if drawn by a homing device.

When she stopped at his feet and he put a warm hand on her shoulder, she trembled, but this time with a jolt of desire. He helped her to her feet, frowning at the mask. But when he reached for it to tug it off, she stopped him. Shannon appeared at his elbow and whispered in his ear, then shot her a sympathetic glance before disappearing into the gloom.

His dark eyes narrowed, face clouded with a quick-tempered reaction she didn't like. Then he nodded and led her out of the room, down the hall, and into a room lit with one candle. The St. Andrew's Cross stood tall, beckoning her in ways she couldn't comprehend.

When he spoke, Brody's words poured sweet, warm Tennessee honey over her soul. "Now, let's see what I can do for you, mystery woman...." He took off his coat and tie, standing there, perfect as ever, and waited for her to do her part.

Chapter Six

Brody's brain burned. He was convinced that if he caught sight of himself in a mirror, actual flames would be rising off his scalp. What a fan-fucking-tastic moment.

The woman stood before him, face half covered by a mask he'd not liked at first, until he decided he did like it, because it gave her a mysterious aura, like a puzzle, his to solve. He sensed the lusty waves emanating from her as if he were a superhero possessed of such ability. Lovely, creamy, rich-looking bare skin tempted him. She was fleshier, shorter, less angular than his usual type. But that made her all the more intriguing.

He licked his lips, took a few steps toward her, and drew her hand to his mouth, kissing it before leading her to the St. Andrew's cross. Gently, he fastened her wrists, and let his fingertips trail down the underside of her arms, across the tops of her breasts, and to her waist. Then, lower, to her thighs, calves and ankles. He got on all fours and gently kissed the top of each of her feet that were encased in shiny fuck-me pumps.

He worked his slow, pleasant way back up, teasing the insides of her legs, just grazing the outside of a pair of black panties. He tingled from his head to his toes, but most especially right below his belt. Grinning, but holding back an odd sort of whooshing noise that was hovering around the edge of his consciousness, he stepped away, loving how she writhed and tugged against her restraints.

He'd never taken the time to observe a woman like this. The concept that women, and some men, had come here as honest-to-god submissives felt strange, but it had to be the biggest turn-on he'd experienced in his entire life, at least the part of it he remembered. He shook his head, not allowing any kind of stupid memory-witch—as he'd come to call the redhead who haunted him daily—ruin this for him. Nope. He wanted to go all out tonight and see how this

Domination thing really worked. No more spank-the-random-girl-while-he-fucked-her and Amber got to watch.

Mystery woman sighed, drawing attention back to his task. Forcing a go-slow approach in order to savor the sensation of her smooth, hot skin, he ran his fingers up her sides, across the tops of her breasts, and up her neck. Transfixed for a moment by the sight of the pulse beating in her long, lovely throat, he leaned in and pressed his lips to it, the sensation both erotic and enervating.

The onrush of more memories almost left him collapsed in a heap at the bound woman's feet. But he willed both of them to relax. When their lips met and she allowed his tongue to probe and explore, his brain exploded with a vision so clear and bright he whimpered. He cradled her face. Tasted the tang of her tears.

Forcing himself to end the kiss, he stepped away, unable to catch his breath. Images rushed at him full force, blinding him to the lovely woman in front of him. He pressed the heels of his hands to his eyes.

As quickly as they appeared, the memories vanished, snuffed out like a candle flame. His body roared into action, propelling him forward. He was determined to be what the masked woman needed him to be. Not weak, sniveling, whining, and useless. Not tonight.

He put his hand on a table that contained several instruments, a flogger, an alarming black leather bullwhip, nipple clamps, choosing the only thing that seemed familiar. He trailed the flogger along her shoulders and breasts, smiling when she shivered, mesmerized once again by the pulse beat in her neck. She stayed quiet a long time, this mysterious treasure chest begging for him to unlock.

Flicking her thighs and stomach with the soft leather, loving the small noises it drew from her throat, he watched as her creamy skin reddened under his attention. A raw, animal-like power rose in him and on its heels, lust so keen it was painful. He put his hand on the erection under his dress trousers, pondering what in the hell he wanted anymore.

What makes you think you can do this? Why should this beautiful woman trust you?

Clutching the flogger's handle in a death grip, he dropped to his heels against the wall. Pain bloomed in him, everywhere and nowhere. At once awful and wonderful, and on the heels of that, an anger so intense he gasped. Confusion warred with intent. Fury battled with remorse, all bracketed by a cavernous loneliness that made his chest ache.

"Use it."

Brody looked up, startled by the sound of her voice. The woman's full lips parted, and she spoke again.

"Use what you're feeling right now. Don't question it. Go with your gut."

He stepped up to his mystery woman, bound, spread, and at his mercy, and ran his hand up her arm to her neck, pondering how she'd sensed his panic. How her words prompted him to untie her and run away before he did something truly irreversible. Emotions he rejected burbled up to his surface, as he trembled with uncertainty, which pissed him off, and sent another shaft of pain and pleasure through his skull.

"Who are you," he whispered, licking his way up the long line of her neck. She exuded some sort of aura that almost forced him to his knees. To submit...to Her. The red headed devil woman—she was here in the room with him.

He blinked as the anger he repressed colored his vision. This cunt who haunted his nightly attempts at sleep with her taunts and jabs and whips stood before him, at his fucking mercy.

He tightened his hand on the bitch's arm and grabbed the bullwhip from the table. Unfurling it, he grimaced as his body raced ahead while his mind resisted. He'd be the boss in this room, and this bitch had to pay for making him so miserable. For using him and turning him into a whiny little boy. The sound of the loud crack of the whip splitting the air frightened him, then spurred him forward.

When her cry of pain ripped through his subconscious, he stopped. His vision blurred. When it returned to normal he saw what he'd done to his submissive. The woman's skin glowed red where he striped her. He glimpsed his hand, white-knuckled on the whip's handle. Sweat dripped into one eye.

What happened? He remembered nothing after picking up the whip and facing her, his enemy. His Mistress.

He dropped the instrument with a cry, and stumbled back, tripping and falling to the floor. The horror of what he'd done to a complete stranger that his stupid, fucked-up brain convinced him to whip relentlessly hit him, bringing a rush of nausea. The red-headed bitch who held him hostage, body and soul. But when?

"Fuck! Shit. Goddamn it." He pounded his forehead with a fist, as if that would force lurking, scrabbling memories just under the surface of his stubborn brain to the light of day. "Why can't I remember anything?"

A loud sob broke his concentration. He scrambled to his knees across from the bound, bleeding, and crying woman. Then half-crawled, half-ran to her, his fingers hovering over her damaged legs—damage he had caused in some kind of trance state. The classroom appeared again as clear as day, her at the front, done up like a Dominatrix for a movie, all leather-clad, high-booted, masked, and sexy as hell. But for the words spilling from her bright red lips.

"You're my bitch, Brody. My toy. Mine. If I catch you ogling sorority girls again, you'll regret it for the rest of your stupid life, do you understand?"

He opened his mouth to speak, but before he uttered a word, she had him pinned beneath her. They were both naked. Except for a heavy leather collar that choked him every time he tried to take a full breath and a mask over his eyes. But he felt her, fucking him, taking what she wanted while he just laid there and let her.

She tugged the chain connecting the clamps to his nipples. "Oh baby! Now! Now, Brody!"

He heard her yell as his cue. But for what?

He tried to focus on the here and now. To help the poor, innocent person he'd whipped so hard as her ragged sobs filled their private room. He had hurt her. He unlatched the wrist restraints, flipped open the ankle bonds, surprised when she collapsed into his arms calling him Robert over and over again. He went with his gut and picked her up, cradled her to his chest, making nonsense sounds he hoped were comforting.

Phantom, long-forgotten pain, and a deep, toothache-like agony settled in his shoulder. The shoulder he had to have manipulated by team therapists daily. She had done that. That bitch had restrained him for a day, a whole twenty-four-hour period, his arms yanked up over his head and fastened into cuffs that dangled from her ceiling. An entire day he hung there, punishment for flirting with a girl not His Mistress in a hallway of his dorm at Vanderbilt.

He gasped.

The woman in his arms had her face buried in his neck, her arms around him. He held onto her, cursing his rock-hard cock, his stupid lizard brain that still wanted to fuck, even after all this. Something about the pain memory made him yearn for a connection. He glanced down at mystery woman's legs, a horrible angry red, thanks to him. He touched one of the ugly marks. She flinched but didn't let him go.

He tilted her face up, thumbed the mask, and pondered taking it off, but then she had her lips on his, kissing him so hard he lost track of everything. He broke from her, puzzled but with a renewed focus, and reached for the bowl of condoms on the bedside table as she eased off her panties. She smiled, and took the foil packet from him, tossing it over his shoulder before leaning in to own his mouth again.

Keeping their lips locked, he lifted her off his lap and down on to the soft, silky bed cover. "Who are you?" he asked when he was naked, between her legs, then inside her body.

They cried out in unison when he stroked deep, as his entire existence coalesced into this moment with this woman. She shuddered and tightened around him, groaning as she climaxed.

"Who are you," he demanded again, propped up with one hand while reaching for her mask with the other. But she stopped him.

"Come, Robert. Come now."

Her request triggered a reaction he'd never experienced. His face burned at a sudden bizarre flash of realization at who she must be. The release roared up from the depths of his soul, he moaned and obeyed her, tears dropping onto her skin. "I'm sorry," he said. "Sophie. I'm so, so sorry." His voice rasped in his ears as he spoke, confusion and remorse and loss all forcing more tears. Sophie. Why had he used that name?

"It's okay." She cradled him close, their bodies still connected, sweat slicking their skin.

She stroked his hair, and for the first time in his memory a one-hundred-percent sense of rightness suffused him. His memory was a sketchy, elusive thing, but he let it go and allowed it to just be.

She stirred, and he dropped down to his side when she got up and retreated to the bathroom. "Don't go. Please."

She shook her head, keeping her back to him then turned, and he saw a tear fall from under that stupid mask.

Within a few minutes, she stood over him, re-dressed in dark jeans, black boots, and a silky blouse. His heart pounded. Something like abject terror made him want to run out of the room. But he stayed still. Whoever she was, she'd come here to get what he gave her, nothing more or less. Embarrassment at his behavior rolled through him. He tried once more before he allowed the ugly side of him to rear up and take him over again.

"Please?" he asked, holding out a hand.

She hesitated, seemingly frozen at the sight of his outstretched palm, then reached out her hand. A sickening sense of déjà vu enveloped him. He'd seen her like this before, taking his hand in a situation that was awkward, but made better by this simple act.

Their hands met. He tugged her, wanting her close, somehow knowing this as their move, their secret body language of...could it be love? This was them, together? He wanted nothing so badly as to be with her.

"Sophie," he repeated.

"No." She yanked away. He stared at the door she slammed behind her then sat up, a nauseating pain holding his skull in a vise. He grabbed his phone still lying on top of the clothes in a heap at his feet. He didn't even remember taking them off.

"Come get me," he whispered after hitting Amber's speed dial.

He wasn't sure how long he lay on the bed, huddled under a silky cover. But eventually, Amber appeared at the door, helped him get dressed, and led him out of the club. She'd accompanied him there, agreeing to let him explore. All he wanted now was to sleep, perhaps never to wake again. A bone-deep loneliness suffused him. With something like desperation, he touched her arm, grateful, despite his overall misgivings about her as a person.

"Thanks," he muttered, then remembered nothing else until she woke him when they'd arrived at his condo and helped him into bed.

• • • •

THE BALLS CAME AT HIM, the cleated players pounded around him, the crowd roared. Sweat blinded him. He was on a soccer pitch, no, the inside of a classroom, then in a random locker room familiar for so many years to him with its noise and stink. Then, the dark-paneled club, filled with attractive people seeking strangers to spank, and whip, and fuck in exchange for a few hundred bucks.

The game...the game...focus, you meathead.

He flinched, his shoulder singing out in agony. The players rushed him, all wearing Her face, her evil grin. That bitch of a professor at Vanderbilt who'd ruined him for anything like a normal relationship. Except for Sophie.

The name slammed him in the gut. She had been normal for him, special, wonderful. He had loved her.

Blinking as the cool night breeze caressed his face and wound around his naked skin, he sensed his body's readiness, the sharpness of his mind, as he crouched on the top of the balcony's ledge. If he didn't do this, he would go insane and take everything and everyone with him. The mostly deserted suburban street mocked him. His Mistress waited down there, smiling her horrible smile, her huge green eyes sharp with purpose.

She unfurled her whip, the one he'd been a slave to for so long. Why? Why had he been drawn to such a manipulative person? Someone who hurt him then pleased him until he no longer understood how to experience pain or pleasure.

He grimaced at the pain in his shoulder again. His arms were over his head. He clutched a metal railing, leaned out over the fancy landscaping, taking in the trees that would likely break his fall, along with his arms and legs. Pain blinded him. It was centered in his groin, his shoulder, and the back of his head. His dick was hard, in that sick correlation of pain/pleasure he'd been programmed to accept. He didn't understand. He hated it, hated himself and the girl sleeping in his bed. Right now, there seemed only one way to fix it.

He put out a bare foot. Let it dangle in the air. He loosened his grip on the overhead railing as gravity pulled him forward.

The mystery woman had abandoned him, His Mistress had intervened and forced her away. He had nothing, wanted nothing, but an end to the round robin of sleepless nights, half memories of recent contentment tinged with older ones of abject misery disguised as happiness.

When the hand still gripping the rail went numb, he simply let go, marveling at how easy that step had been.

"Brody!" a female voice screamed. Someone grabbed at him, yanked him close, pulling him down to the balcony floor. "Baby, baby, what are you doing? My god." She held him, the woman who saved him, who cared about him and took care of him. She rocked him, crooning in comfort.

He stared at her dry-eyed, gut-deep emptiness driving him to a rash decision. "Marry me, Amber," he croaked out.

"Oh course, my love." she said, and he tried hard to ignore the flash of satisfaction on her face before he stood, pulled her up, ripped off her silk pajama shorts, and fucked her on the balcony, all the while feeling absolutely nothing.

Chapter Seven

Sophie winced when the shower water hit her still whip-striped legs. She leaned against the tile, taking deep breaths and internalizing the pain that had been so very worth it. Every blessed strike to her skin had done something she'd required.

Even if it hadn't been Brody doing the whipping, she would have embraced it. She hadn't experienced that sort of punishment—the kind that shoved her deep into subspace—in years. Frank had been good with the whip and as sick as that whole thing had been, she missed portions of it. The part of her that needed to be centered, to not be in charge, to surrender all control for a few glorious moments of pain and pleasure, had been empty for years.

Tonight, the new-and-not-terribly improved Brody had fulfilled her in ways she loved. She'd gone so deep in to her private space, into the glorious quiet. All she knew was the crack-snap of the whip on her flesh. She'd been surprised when he stopped, then when the pain hit her in the next second, she understood why he had.

Sensing his extreme distress from across the room, she'd lost it. That's why she cried. Not from pain. Pain had released her in a way she'd missed. She'd obviously been in deep denial about that particular piece of her personality. But Brody...Robert...had been so distraught by the sight of her, it broke what remained of her heart.

She'd known it was him within seconds. Something in her had shoved her forward, forced her to take action. Leading to the most erotic moment of her life. When he'd slipped into her body, whispering her name as if fantasizing, making careful, perfect love to her, something broken in her had simply healed.

And that allowed her to take the final step away from him. Because she had fully intended to remove the mask, to confront him and tell him who she was, and what they had created together. To tell him about his son.

But she'd collected that back to herself, got dressed and ready to leave. Then at the last minute, when he'd held out his hand, open-palmed, like he used to, she made her final decision. Brody was lost to her. She had to let him go.

"Mommy!" The sound of Sam's voice echoed through the bathroom, startling her. "Let's go! We're gonna miss the practice!"

She sighed, got out, and toweled off. It had been nearly a week since her moment at the club. Susan had given her some salve to put on the wounds. While she yearned for something similar, for a heart salve, a memory bandage, so that all thoughts and visions of her time with Robert J. Vaughn might actually be covered up and eventually healed.

Susan knew everything—about Katrina's, Frank, and even Brody. It had been the best kind of relief to have such a friend she trusted and unburdened to. After that night, she'd convinced Sophie to stay home a couple of days, calling in sick but doing a ton of stuff from her laptop. When Saturday had arrived, she'd decided to head in, figuring she'd use the off-weekend for the team to let Sam run around while she got some work done.

Her phone buzzed, and she grabbed it as she brushed out her wet hair. The fragile inner peace she'd maintained since the encounter at the club was shattered to bits by the text from Jack:

Brody is out. Getting married to that bitch of an agent and she's demanding we honor his request for transfer to Boston.

• • • •

THIS IS FOR THE BEST, she said to herself for the millionth time. He's gone anyway. Your Brody is never coming back, no matter that one brief glimpse of him you got that night. Let him take this step. Clinging to him by pretending to wait for the best offer is immature. Grow up. Move on for good.

Sophie reviewed the ten-page document she'd drawn up, frowning at the price they were getting for the man—the sort of figure that seemed unreal, pretend, and would allow them to purchase a new goalkeeper at a slightly lower salary than what Brody currently commanded.

All good for the Black Jacks.

All good for Sophie.

All good.

Her gaze fell on the thick, creamy envelope with the fancy calligraphy spelling out her full name. She squeezed her eyes shut, willing it away. The whole team had been invited to the wedding at the Grosse Pointe Yacht Club. It would be the social event of the year, attended by soccer celebrities, sports commentators, crawling with photographers and gossipmongers. It would be a lovely, horrible event. She swept the stupid thing into the trash and refocused on the contract, ignoring the serendipity of the wedding date set for Brody Vaughn and Amber London: June tenth. The day his son turned four.

She drifted, revisiting some of the more erotic moments she'd shared with the young man who had captured her heart and still gripped it so tight she could sense the warmth of his hand.

The distinct sound of a throat clearing behind her forced her gaze from the empty soccer field below. She blinked, shocked to find none other than Brody's fiancée, Amber, standing there, cutting Sophie with her sharp stare. She sighed and leaned back in her seat.

"Can I help you?" she asked, making sure her tone stayed clipped and businesslike

"I need to tell you something." The woman took a seat without being invited.

Sophie glared at the pushy, successful woman on the verge of fulfilling her dream, that of owning the Brody Vaughn brand by transforming herself into Missus Vaughn.

"I'm busy." She stared down at her desk, setting her jaw, the words on various papers blurring. No way this woman would make her cry.

"I don't think you'll be too busy for this."

The woman tossed something down on the tidy desk, giving her an eye-popping view of the obnoxious huge diamond on her left ring finger. She frowned at the paper. It bore the letterhead of Nathan Gage, PI and fully outlined a report she skimmed until fixating on two things. Proprietor of an illegal prostitution ring, Katrina's. And, follow-up report to child protective services as to the safety of Samuel Robert Harrison.

Her brain refused to accept it. She forced herself to meet Amber's steely gaze. "What is this about?" She tried not to scream or plant her fist right into the expensively perfected nose.

"I know that kid is Brody's," Amber said, her casual attitude familiar, that of the shark-agent using her best weapon. Pretending that whatever happened during negotiations didn't really matter. That she would win, no matter what.

"I don't care what you think you know," Sophie declared, her ears ringing with terror. "There's nothing illegal about Katrina's. It's not prostitution. It's a fully licensed, bonded, and insured dating service. You're bluffing."

"Funny thing about the media, though," Amber gave her a wide fake grin. "They're kinda lazy." She put both hands on the desk. Light bounced off the diamond, blinding Sophie for a split second. She leaned in close, as if they were gal pals exchanging gossip over coffee. "Consider this is my insurance policy."

Sophie opened her mouth to tell the woman to get her filthy, lying, blackmail report off her desk and never come back. Amber held up a finger, waggling it like a teacher in the face of a naughty student.

"Brody is mine. I'm getting him the hell away from you and your stupid club on purpose. I'm losing money, too, which I don't like to do because I know if I let him play another season here...." She waved a dismissive hand at the window with its view of the team practice. The view Sophie loved and hated all at once. "He'd likely command even more dough." She crossed her arms, meeting Sophie's incredulous gaze.

"I want my fiancé as far from you and your love-child, over-the-hill influence as I can get him. No questions asked."

"But we're about to sign this," Sophie spluttered, anger and a lick of fear darkening her vision. "I mean, we agree to your terms. We're letting him go." She stopped talking, and rose, wanting to feel above this grasping, desperate excuse for a woman. "So take your blackmail bullshit and stuff it up your bony ass. I let Brody go years ago. Some of us know how to behave like mature humans, to understand when we just aren't going to get our way, no matter how badly we want it. Go, marry him, cheat on him, let him cheat on you, and have a messy public divorce. I don't care."

She walked around her desk and yanked the door open. "Next time, make an appointment to see me. I'm way too busy for your nonsense." Her knees shook. But she kept her voice calm and neutral.

The other woman stood, never taking her eyes from Sophie's. "I'll go." She sneered. "And I'm leaving this with you, so you always remember that any time you get the urge to pretend to be a sub when my Brody is at a club, or anything remotely sneaky just to get near him again." She picked up the paper with thumb and forefinger and waved, then dropped it. "This shit gets real, Katrina."

Sam chose that second to burst through the door, clutching his Black Jack-branded soccer ball. Amber's smile narrowed at the sight of him—the so-painfully obvious mini-Brody. The boy stopped, then stuck out his small hand. "Hello. I'm Sam Harrison. Nice to meet you."

Amber crouched down and contemplated Sam for about a second too long for Sophie's inner mama bear to tolerate. She stepped between him and Amber. The woman rose, her smirk back in place.

"Such a handsome young man. No doubt great at soccer, too. So nice to meet you Sam," she said, her gaze fixed on Sophie. "You take care now. Be a good boy for your mommy." And in a flash of white teeth, she exited the office.

Sophie crumpled into one of the side leather chairs.

Sam, in his usual, too-mature-for-his-own-good way, gripped her wrist. "Mommy, what's wrong? Is she a bad lady? I think she might be."

She took a breath. Gathering the boy close, she tried not to scare him by crying or screaming. He let her hold him for a minute, then patted her hair and wiggled out of her grasp, his usual nervous energy getting the best of him. He climbed up on the window ledge, standing with his nose pressed to the glass. She was breathless with terror at the thought of losing him.

But she got up and sat with him, her amazing creation, while he called out encouragement down to the field where the grown men scrimmaged.

Chapter Eight

Just ten days to go and all this wedding hoopla would be behind him. He'd be on his way to a new team in a more established market, new town, new life, new everything, including new reality—that of married man. As his teammates jostled and joked and fucked around in the locker room, Brody maintained his usual independence, once more part of, but not really included in, their friendly bullshit. With one foot out the door anyway, he had no idea why he even showed up to practice. Other than his desire to stay with them.

He sighed and turned to stare into his locker. Since the moment Amber pulled him back from the brink, and he'd done the one thing he thought he'd never do, his life had taken on a level of strangeness that seemed detached from him.

Amber had him in front of tux makers, florists, bakers, caterers, DJs, limo services, photographers, videographers, the works. They picked out her engagement ring together, settling on the biggest one possible, it seemed. But he didn't care. He would watch her at night while she slept, wondering who she even was, other than the one thing that kept his tenuous sanity together by its short hairs.

At times, he hated her. Truly despised pretty much everything about her, including her bossy snarkiness, her casual dismissal of his one expressed desire not to leave the Black Jacks, her skinny ass, her bony hips. But he fucked her a lot. Jesus wept. Did they fuck a lot. His cock felt raw when shower water hit it.

Despite that, he'd leap at her every chance he got, rip her clothes, and plow into her like an animal. He had no idea why. Other than it kept him from having to actually converse with her.

He dried off, put on his suit, and wandered out into the spring evening. The latest task he'd been given—to locate five men to stand with him and one to be his best man, had knocked him for a complete loop. He had no idea what that even meant. He had no close friends. So he'd started pondering and rejecting various team members.

"Hey, Vaughn!" He blinked, confused, his head starting to ache from lack of food. Metin lingered in the doorway. "Can I talk to you?"

He nodded and followed the coach back into the complex. They sat, gripping water bottles, staring at each other. Brody had no reason to think he'd done anything wrong, no reason for Metin to call some kind of impromptu meeting with him. He leaned back, taking in the single photo gracing the small desk that sat under a window in the office. Metin smiling down at a baby, while an attractive dark-haired woman held it in her arms. He shuddered. Kids. God. He had no plans to impregnate Amber. No fucking way.

Metin cleared his throat. Brody dragged his gaze from the photo. "Listen, Vaughn, I wanted to check on you. Make sure you're okay with how, ah, fast things are moving for you right now."

Brody nodded, sipped his water, still missing the point of this meeting.

"I'm living proof that a woman's love can save you," his coach said, surprising him. "You know my story. If it had not been for Melanie, for my wife, I wouldn't be sitting here in any way, shape, or form as a normal human being."

He took a deep breath, processing the man's words.

"So, I just want you to know that... um... I think you're making a mistake. Marrying Amber."

"Not your business, I guess," he said, suddenly angry.

"Actually it is. I feel responsible for you. We recruited you away from a going-nowhere team. I like to think I taught you a few things. You helped make the Black Jacks what they are today. I didn't want to trade you and fought it because I don't think you want to go. I think you're leaving for the wrong reasons. Those reasons all center around one person: Amber London. She doesn't want you here. And while I know why...I...."

Brody sucked in a breath. "What do you know, exactly?" Something simmered between the two men. Brody sensed unspoken words burning a hole in Metin's throat. Words he wanted to say, but couldn't or wouldn't, for whatever reason.

"Listen, Brody." Metin set his empty water bottle on the table next to the photo, letting his gaze rest on it for a few seconds.

The pure emotion in the other man's expression hit him hard. Brody narrowed his eyes, something tickling the back of his brain. He leapt up and began to pace.

"I'm fine," he insisted. "I'll be fine. Whatever it is you aren't telling me probably shouldn't be said. I need to go." He stumbled out, climbed on his bike, and roared off, not paying attention to anything but forward motion, running hard and fast away from a truth that lurked around the edges of his life but that he simply wouldn't—or couldn't—acknowledge.

• • • •

ONE WEEK LATER, HE'D lined up some players as groomsmen and had asked Metin to be his best man. The coach had smiled, clapped Brody on the shoulder, and said he'd be honored. No sign of the meeting, or the fact of Metin's disapproval of his fiancée remained between them. He had an appointment with the legal lady, which he anticipated with an inappropriate amount of excitement. Then, remembering the reason for the meeting, he sighed and climbed off the bike, stashing his helmet and pushing his sunglasses up on his head.

It would be his last time with her, his last official day in this building. He'd cleaned out his locker, taken his nameplate off the front of it with a sort of bemused detachment. He had no control over his life anymore, which on some levels gave him relief. Someone did. Amber, soon to be his wife, held the reins and looked out for his best interests. He sighed, wishing that whatever had been niggling at him since Metin had done his little don't marry her thing would reveal itself.

His footfalls echoed in the hall. Familiar smells of new building, new turf, and plenty of sweat wafted across his senses. His heart pounded and his body headed into a weird fight-or-flight mode. Simultaneously sweaty, cold, antsy, and stressed in a way he hated, he would give anything to have Amber there handling this. But she had a fitting or some shit for her dress and wanted to go out with her giant posse of girlfriends afterward. Sophie and Jack had requested his presence today, a Saturday, a few days before he got married. He shook his head, dispelling doubts for the millionth time in the last few weeks.

He turned the corner, his mind running a thousand miles a minute, and felt something bump straight into his lower legs. He grabbed the wall and nearly fell down on top of a kid who was sitting on his butt, rubbing his forehead and frowning. Brody stared at the boy.

He'd seen him before, hanging around practices. Nicco gave him shoulder rides, and the others would kick around with him as if he were somehow a part of them. He had longish, jet-black hair and was wearing a small replica of the Black Jack's uniform shirt, jeans that were grass-stained at the knees, plus flat, indoor soccer shoes. Brody crouched down to get on his level.

"Sorry little dude," he said, then took a step back when the boy glared at him, his mind frozen with something like recognition.

Brody had found an old shoebox that contained what he assumed were photos of himself a few days ago. It had been at the bottom of his closet, almost hidden. He'd dragged it out and sat with his back to the wall, thumbing through its contents.

Photos, mostly cheap Polaroids, faded to nearly gone. A few actually from film, developed in the old way before camera phones and digital processing put the Kodaks of the world nearly out of business. One in particular floated across his vision at that moment, of him about five maybe, or four years old, his dark hair flopped over his forehead, double-dimpled, clutching a no-doubt dead frog and grinning a huge, toothy smile at whoever snapped the picture.

He stared at the boy's face now in front of him, soccer ball cradled in his arms like a precious treasure and experienced the most bizarre sensation—that of gazing into a time-traveling mirror.

The boy's eyes darkened. Brody watched as the kid's anger warred with his politeness training. His heart seemed to skip a few beats when the kid got to his feet, tucked the ball under one foot like a mini expert, and stuck out his hand. Brody swallowed hard and took it. The warmth from the boy's small palm gave him the oddest urge to sweep him up into his arms.

"Sorry. I wasn't looking where I was going." His voice sounded a million miles away. The large, carpeted hall disappeared, faded to nothing but the two of them. He and this astonishing, small version of him. He finally let go, realizing he'd been crouched down, gawking at the kid for too long.

"Sam!" a familiar female voice called out. The boy stepped back, his small face confused. His ball rolled away from them and Brody snagged it, popped it up into the air, then tucked it under his arm. He held out a hand to his side, somewhat surprised when the boy took it.

"Where are you?" the female voice continued.

"Sounds like you're in trouble. Let's go get you out of it."

The boy nodded solemnly, his face splitting into a heart-stopping grin when Brody winked at him. They walked hand-in-hand toward the sound of the woman's voice. His pulse raced when he caught sight of Sophie, the legal lady he'd rough fucked on her desk that one time. She took his random, good-natured flirtation well afterwards, and he admired that. But she also populated some of his more erotic, yet intensely emotional, dreams. The oddest sensation hit him when she spotted them, him and the boy, together. That of relief.

"Sam!" She jumped for them, yanking the kid away as if he were the creepy dude in the van with candy. "Where have you been? You know you aren't allowed to roam around like...like that."

Sam protested. "Mommy! I was just...he is..." The boy stared at him, pleading wordlessly for Brody to help him out of the oncoming jam.

"Sorry, Sophie," he said, shrugging. "We were kicking the ball around in the hall. I distracted him, I guess." He straightened, trying to dispel the eerie vision that flashed through his mind.

Sophie, him, in bed, her smell and taste, her words in his ear, soothing and calming him, a vision so clear he had to clench his fists to stop from grabbing her and holding her close. But her eyes were flat, emotionless, so he figured he'd projected something forbidden. Something he might want but would never have.

Besides, he was an engaged man, practically a husband. He grimaced at that realization. He crouched down to the kid standing beside his mother's legs. "How old are you, Sam?" The question surprised everyone.

"I'm almost four." The little boy's chest puffed up. "My birthday is...."

But Sophie stepped into the middle of the conversation shoving Sam behind her and glaring at Brody. "His birthday is coming up and none of your business. You're late. Let's get this over with."

The irrational compulsion to run his finger down her tightly clenched jaw, to kiss her just under her ear, to thread his fingers in the brown tumble of her hair forced Brody to take a step back. He blinked, and it appeared again, this time a more graphic sensation of being connected with her, inside her body, moving together in a perfect, sensuous rhythm.

Jack appeared behind her. She flinched, then frowned again, and the vision vanished like so much smoke. She emanated such distress, such an agonizing level of discomfort, it gave him physical pain to see it.

Unthinking, as if by rote or memory, he touched her upper arm. The entire group of them—Sophie, her son, and Jack Gordon, founder of the club, observed quietly as his hand moved lower, trailing down to her elbow, to her wrist. Unable, perhaps unwilling, to stop, he put her fingers to his lips. He felt her shaking, sensed her son's gaze on him, registered the boy's open-mouthed stare. He only wished to soothe, to drive that expression of terrified unhappiness off her beautiful face. Jack cleared his throat. Brody and Sophie took a step away from each other.

"Mommy?" Sam's small, confused voice broke through his dream state.

She tugged out of his grip. Then the surprise on her face morphed immediately into resignation. "Come on," she said, turning away. "Let's get this shit done."

Chapter Nine

Sophie's legs shook, but she marched back the few yards to her door, heart pounding and face flushed with anger. She stood, braced in the doorway with both hands, surveying the scene. Her large, luxurious office with its open workspace, subtle lamp lighting, cushy leather seats, Turkish rugs, and giant glass wall mocked her. She sighed, mentally rewinding the last hour of shocking news and even more earth-shattering encounters.

It had begun innocuously enough. She'd anticipated the final meeting with Brody without too much angst. Ever since Amber lobbed the threat at her with Sam's name splashed all over that bogus report about Sophie's other life, she'd been slowly coming to terms with the fact that she had to let Brody go.

She had all she needed now—her son, her careers, money, and security, along with several good friends, now that she counted Jack Gordon and his wife Sara among them. Would be nice to get laid, or even just share a romantic dinner with a man again someday. But she figured that might materialize, eventually.

Now that she'd resumed her focus, the one she lost after Evan, and Frank, and now Brody, men were off her to-do list. Well, unless she jumped back into her role as chief Dominatrix—highly unlikely.

Arriving with Sam in tow had not been on the agenda today. She'd been irritated by him since early morning when he did his usual rise-at-the-crack-of-dawn and jump into her bed, stating his intent to go with her to the soccer place. She'd groaned and rolled over, gathered him close, buried her nose in his neck, willing him to sleep for a few more minutes. He had allowed entrapment for a few moments. Then wiggled free with a squeal and a bounce.

"You're not going with me today, Sam." She'd trudged to the bathroom.

I love my child, I swear it. But god help me if he doesn't learn to sleep past six a.m. soon.

"Yes I am, Mommy. You gots a message on the phone. Jen is sick today and can't play with me while you're at the soccer place."

"Why are you listening to my phone messages, Samuel?" she asked, climbing out of the shower and drying off. Sam was lounged on her bed with his cat and Legos, crafting an elaborate Gulliver's Travels-style siege on the poor animal.

He never glanced up from his plastic-toy attack. "Because I saw her name. So I listened." His matter-of-factness made her smile in spite of her annoyance of the main message: she had to take Sam with her. On this of all days, the day she said goodbye to the boy's father over a contract, in a bizarre reversal of the way they'd met. She'd stared at herself in the mirror, wishing for nothing more than for Brody to know about his son.

Too late for that now, of course, she'd reasoned, pulling on clothes and fastening her hair up as Sam got louder and more excited about his field trip to Detroit. Exhausted in body and spirit, she'd put oatmeal in front of him and threw some coloring books and toys in a backpack, along with granola bars and bananas so he wouldn't nag her about his ever-empty stomach.

God help her but she had no energy to deal with her son today. His chattering, singing, banging crap around on the table brought nothing but aggravation. She gritted her teeth from her spot inside the pantry closet.

Adding the keep-up-with and keep-Sam-entertained element to the anticipated drama of her day made her nearly physically ill. Or want to cry. She did neither, choosing instead to yell at him when his oatmeal bowl ended up on the floor and his milk all over the table. He'd responded back the same way, then cleaned it up in sullen silence.

When they finally got to the soccer complex, she'd been ready to put the kid out on the side of the road. He acted like he was on a sugar high or something. She bit her tongue against the urge to tell him to please shut up, to please give her some peace and quiet. That today of all days, mommy needed some space to think and to process what was about to happen.

He hit the asphalt running, kicking his ball in front of him, his strong, jean-clad legs pumping, his dark hair blown by the spring wind. He needed a haircut, she observed idly. Then stopped, the extreme déjà vu of that simple thought making her dizzy. Shouldering her briefcase, she herded her son into the building, relieved when they ran into Metin, who had his little girl with him, headed out to run around the perimeter of the field.

Surrendering Sam into Metin's capable and less-irritable hands, she started for the elevator. The anticipation of the final meeting with Brody had her in such a snit, she could hardly stand herself. Since she'd skipped her second cup of tea in an effort to get Sam dressed and ready, she stopped at the kiosk that fronted the sidewalk and did brisk business inside and out of the complex. Reinforced by the rich Earl Grey aroma, she walked down the long hall toward the elevators up to the executive suites, greeting the usual cadre of marketing and sales staff, trying not to sound stressed.

Today had portent. The air seemed heavy with it. It pissed her off and at that point she wanted the damn paper signed and Robert J. Vaughn out of her life and onto his new one in Boston with the bitchy Missus.

She opened her door, shocked to see Jack there already, sipping coffee and reading something on his tablet computer. Dropping her briefcase on the desk, she suppressed a shiver of irritation. She required a few minutes alone. Was that so fucking much to ask? But she sipped and waited for her boss to impart his daily dose of wisdom.

He put the tablet down and tented his fingers, staring at her thoughtfully. He'd dressed in his usual, suited best, silky tie in its perfect knot, thick, black hair smooth, his extreme togetherness marred only by a shadow of uncharacteristic stubble on his jaw. That one detail jarred her, being so out of the ordinary for him, enough so she had a moment of worry. Then he spoke, bringing actual anxiety to the table.

"I'm going to nominate you to be general manager at next month's board meeting," he said, his voice neutral as if he'd just recited the weather forecast.

"What?" She set her cup down before she dropped it onto the expensive carpet. "I'm not...you're...where are you going?" He'd started this whole thing and had spearheaded it for the past few years with a boundless energy and enthusiasm. She'd noticed the last time she'd been with him and his wife at a fundraiser, Sara had been quieter than normal, pensive, observing her husband as if he were a stranger. "Is everything okay?"

Jack took a deep breath. "Not really. But I'm dealing with it. Plus, I've got a new wrinkle. Just something I've been asked to consider." He broke their eye contact and gazed out over the soccer pitch where Metin was herding Sam and his little girl around. The sight of her son contented her for a half second. Until she remembered what Jack had said. She leaned back in her chair.

"I can't be GM. Rafe should be."

"He has the soccer background." Jack ran a hand down his face. "But you're all-around the most professional one in the building. Rafe is a great guy. I love having him as a brother-in-law and working with Metin on recruiting. I'm recommending him as head of Soccer Operations. Sort of the COO, if you will." He shot her a serious look. "You are the only one I'd trust to do this. You can hire however many assistants you need or want, and get a new legal department. But Sophie, please consider it. You deserve it and one thing I don't do is recommend promotions for no reason. You would be a great GM for this club."

She frowned, sensing a whole lot of words unsaid behind his little speech. "What's going on with you, Jack? You love this job." He and his wife had met as agents at the highly successful real estate company in Ann Arbor they now owned. "Is it Brandis?" She didn't want to bring it up, but it wasn't a secret that Jack's son had been in trouble.

"No. Well, sort of." Jack shot her a bemused look. "Boys are horrible beasts. I would know, I guess, having been one." He took a breath. "I've been asked to run for office. Considered it long enough to allow Sara to threaten to move out if I added one more project to my personal plate. And you know her well enough to realize as much as I do, that is no joke."

"No, I'm guessing she had her reasons though. What office? Dog catcher?" She kept her voice light.

Jack nodded, chuckling without much humor. "She puts up with a lot from me, no doubt. And this latest thing. Well, it's senator, actually." He shook his head. "Fucking crazy talk."

The light in his eyes had sharpened, and Sophie guessed it resembled the same one Sara had seen years ago when he'd first been asked to explore the possibility of pursuing the new soccer expansion league for a team in Detroit, which had worked out pretty damn well. Jack Gordon did nothing half-way, likely leading to his wife's non-idle threat.

"So," he said, refocusing on her. "I am taking several steps back from the fun house here." He waved a arm indicating the soccer world they'd inhabited together for the last few years. "I need to ponder my options, and to give some serious attention to my home life. I have to. I can't lose that. But I also need to know this is being taken care of the way I would do it. No matter how rocky our beginning years ago, I know you're the only one who can do this for me." He smiled and sat back, leaving her a little breathless.

It would mean one thing for certain, something she'd been contemplating already. Giving up her share of Katrina's, becoming a completely silent partner, and letting Dante hire a manager in her place. Perhaps this was a sign that the time had come to finally do that.

She sighed, noted the time, and stood. "I'll think about it." But she was already accepting it in her head. "Let's get ready for Brody, shall we?"

"You should tell him about Sam."

She froze. Susan had recommended it to her once, over a bottle of wine, but never brought the subject up again after Sophie said she didn't want to discuss it. Other than that, no one had brought it up to her since she'd laid down the law all those years ago, fresh from her silly attempt to seduce the poor man, to force him to remember her that ended in a quick, dirty, and wholly amazing fuck right here in this very room.

"No, I shouldn't. Now make yourself useful and go get us some decent coffee."

"Yes, Ma'am."

She smiled as he sauntered out. Then spent a few minutes taking deep breaths, contemplating how she'd dreaded this day, only to have it take a drastic, life-changing new twist. One that didn't entirely displease her, thanks to Jack and his unexpected announcement and offer. Maybe Brody's exit from her life would be a good thing after all. A chill gripped her spine.

She might justify it that way for the rest of her conscious life, but she would never, ever believe it. The time they had spent together, learning each other's weaknesses and strengths and using them in ways that satisfied them both, would never be fully gone from her memory. She would love him until the day she died.

Jack dropped her coffee off and said he'd be back for the meeting. The next time she emerged from the pile of work, finalizing the trades they had planned for the year, nearly another hour had passed. There were a total of five transfers, including Brody's. She still believed Brody was making a huge mistake going to a second tier team in the bigger league, and not just for her own selfish reasons.

They'd managed to fend off offers for several other players and were welcoming a new cast of hopefully calmer characters. Including a Scottish player named Declan at forward. And some guy who was a defensive player, as well as a former male model—stripper if the rumors were to be believed—named Jace, on defense. Good thing, since their defensive line had gotten a little porous and with the new goalkeeper they'd need to...She stopped, smiling at her own thoughts. Hard to believe not six years ago she'd known as much about soccer as she had about, well, being a single parent.

But fear over Amber's threat still lingered. All of this had been her doing, getting him away from Sophie and their son. At that realization, her head snapped up. She grabbed her phone as she walked to the window, noting that the field was now empty. Where the hell had Sam gotten to? At times like these, she truly doubted her sanity, thinking she should mother anything, anyone, especially a boy with his amount of raw energy.

"Shit," she muttered, still fuzzy and half-distracted by all the information she'd been processing. "Sam?" she called out to the outer ring of cubicles.

He sometimes hung out there, watching the many televisions tuned to some soccer game or another. She glanced at her phone, saw a text from Metin saying they'd gone out to the grass field adjacent to the stadium and gotten thoroughly filthy kicking the ball around, but he should be on his way up in the elevator now with some of the folks from marketing.

The sales' suite of offices, with its mini soccer field, boxes of swag, and general air of playroom, always proved tempting. She wandered down there, pondering how the head of that department would take to having her as his boss. Not well. He'd be the first one she'd replace.

Distracted, she came around the corner and saw them, hand-in-hand. Her son and his father, so breathtakingly perfect, she gasped and stumbled back out of their line of sight. She closed her eyes, willing it gone, willing him gone and out of her heart forever. But she had to face this. He'd come up there to sign his release contract. He wanted to move on. She had to let him.

Squaring her shoulders, she called Sam's name and walked back around the corner as if she hadn't already seen them. Her knees shook as she yanked Sam away from Brody. The boy's face dissolved into what she recognized as an imminent tantrum. Jack put a hand on her shoulder, and they all stood there, frozen in a bizarre tableau.

Brody's touch on her arm shocked her. His lips on her fingers had the opposite effect, as if he had poured warm water across her nerves. She wanted to melt into him, like she used to. Soothe and be soothed in the way they had discovered by accident when they tried to play or mess around with bonds and floggers.

Her child's voice jolted her back to reality. "Mommy?" he asked, his face dark and unhappy at the vision of his mother so obviously distraught, and of this man, a stranger, kissing her hand.

She pulled away, not angry, just resigned. "Come on." She turned away from him once and for all, Sam's hand grasped in hers. "Let's get this shit done."

Chapter Ten

Once the contract was signed and the deed accomplished, Brody took a long, deep breath. He would no longer be a Black Jack, a BJ, one of The Gentlemen, as their marketing department tried to spin them. He glanced down at the fists he had clenched in his lap. Then he caught Sam's stare over his coloring book. Something here seemed strange, wrong, off-center.

His head pounded with the sort of pain he hadn't experienced in a while. Like someone or something had his temples in a metal vise and someone else was pounding the back of his head with a sledgehammer. He leaned over his knees, his breathing ragged. A weird sort of panic had him in its clutches.

"You okay?" A small hand landed on his. He jerked his head up to meet Sam's eyes. "Mister? Do you need some water or a bam-aid?"

"No," he whispered, reaching out to touch the boy's cheek. Sam let him do it before jumping away at the sharp intake of breath from behind Sophie's desk. "I'm fine, Sam. Thank you. I should go." He stood.

Everything in him screamed stay, but he had obligations. A fiancée, a new job in Boston, back-up goalie for more money than here, less chance of getting injured. And not a whole hell of a lot of promises about actual playing time. He'd told Amber that wasn't going to fly. She'd given him one of her patented leave it to me and shut up looks, then ignored him until he had to give some sort of approval for yet another aspect of the wedding.

Sam glanced at his mother, who seemed frozen in her seat. To his amazement, the boy wrapped himself around Brody's lower legs. Heart in his throat, face burning, Brody glared at Sophie over the desk, wanting to ask, but terrified of the answer.

Setting her lips in a thin line, she gave an almost imperceptible nod. A tear slid down her face. Brody gripped Sam's arms and peeled him off. The room narrowed again, to him and the boy who stared back at him, his face a scary mirror into a past Brody couldn't remember. He tried to speak, but his throat closed up. Letting the kid go, he stumbled out of the office, his skin ice cold and his face burning hot, the image of Sam's deep gaze and familiar features branded into his psyche.

• • • •

HE FACED THE FOLLOWING set of twenty-four-hour periods in a daze. The movers came the day before the wedding and had him packed up in no time. He wandered through his condo, touching all the cardboard boxes, sipping a single malt scotch his teammates had given him during an impromptu bachelor party the night before. There had been strippers, a live band, booze, food, the works. He'd sat apart from it all, demurring when offered lap dances, no longer caring about anything, definitely not interested in celebrating.

His mind spun, and his head hurt pretty much all day, every day. He slept maybe three hours a night. All he could picture when he closed his eyes was Sophie—her face, her body, her voice. He could even taste her, hear her, sense her skin against his. When he wasn't day or night dreaming about making love to her, about fucking around with her, about simply sitting and cuddling with her, visions of Sam invaded his brain.

He leaned against a box, gripping the glass. After tugging his phone from his pocket, he thumbed through contacts until he found her. Legal Lady. He'd programmed it in after that one hot hook-up. He stared at the set of numbers, wondering what he might say that would make sense.

"Hey, um, this is Brody. Did we have a kid together, and you never told me? Oh, and by the way, when did that happen because the last memories I have are from when you invited me in to your office and let me fuck you, you know, on your desk? Did I knock you up then, or what?"

Good god, Vaughn, get real. That isn't your kid. You barely know the woman and only in her role as head of the team's legal department.

And of course, as if summoned, she appeared in his mind, naked, smiling, sashaying over to him. Her lips moved and formed words he couldn't hear or process. His dick hardened, pissing him off. When his phone buzzed with an actual call, he dropped it, startled out of his near-wet daydream.

The screen indicated that it was, of all people on the planet, Nicolas Garza, the Spaniard who anchored the team and had been so concerned with Brody's well-being for the last few years. If he didn't know the guy already had a steady boyfriend, he'd guess Nicco had the hots for him. He and Parker, their teammate and Nicco's lover, had spearheaded the bachelor party, and both would be standing with him as groomsmen at the wedding.

"Yeah?" he grunted into the phone.

"Hey, you around?"

"I'm around my condo, if that's what you mean." He tried to stretch out his shoulder, which had started aching more and more lately for no obvious reason.

"I'm downstairs. You got a minute?"

He pushed back from the cardboard stack, surprised. "Sure. I'll buzz you up."

He let his teammate in. "Pull up a box," he said, pointing at his distinct lack of furniture. Nicco just stood, glancing around, his face full of anxiety. "Well, what is it? I have to meet Amber in an hour, pre-rehearsal or something."

He propped himself against the wall, his head setting up that odd cacophony of pain, echoes of memory, and a sort of dizzy, off-kilter sensation that was his new normal.

"Listen, Vaughn, I think you need to know something." Nicco glanced down at the floor. Brody waited. "You had a concussion. A bad one, and it was my fault. You sort of went downhill from there. You didn't play for a while, then Nate got hurt at that nightclub, so you started playing again, before you should have."

Brody's vision did a strange blur-out thing then, as he processed his teammate's words. "I don't...r-r-remember," he said, stumbling over the words.

Nicco held up a hand. "Just wait, listen to me a minute. They told us not to do this to you, that you had to move on, that you probably wouldn't ever fully recall your life before the surgery. But I don't care. This is about you, not..." Nicco waved his hand around, indicating the empty condo.

Brody started pacing, dragging fingers through his hair, running them over the quarter-sized scar near the crown of his head, the one he never asked about. Somehow believing it contained a key to a box he should keep firmly locked. "I don't want to hear this."

"You have to," Nicco said, his voice low and firm. "You and Sophie were together. As in you were a couple."

Brody pulled away. "You're crazy. Bat shit, fucking nuts," he croaked out.

Nicco pulled something from his inside jacket pocket, looked at it a minute, then handed it over. Brody stared at Nicco's phone screen a full thirty seconds before his brain registered what he saw.

His gut roiled with nausea at the scary déjà vu of seeing a photo of himself—or some kind of younger, fresher version of the man he met in the mirror every morning. He was wearing a tuxedo and had his arm around none other than the Legal Lady herself. He dropped the phone on top of a moving box. "What happened to me?" he asked, his voice hoarse.

"Concussion, traumatic brain injury, again, partly my fault. You ended up in some kind of scary surgery. The docs opened up your skull, and in the process of saving your life, gave your memories a solid scramble. They can't explain it. Which is why I'm here now. Because you have to know this before you marry that...um, before you marry Amber, and leave the team."

Brody gulped and picked the phone up again. Sophie looked so beautiful in her deep blue dress, smiling for cameras, tucked into his side exactly as he had dreamed. "I'm gonna puke."

He raced for the bathroom. His eyes watered and his chest heaved. He remembered her, heard her words, and saw her mouth move as she spoke them: Your call, stud, but something tells me the closer the better. As if she were there, right then, talking to him. He saw her, tasted her, sensed her body enveloping him.

More words he now remembered: I have something to tell you, flashed in front of his mind. Then, nothing, blackness, a hole he didn't even try to dig out of, so focused he'd been on playing, working out, and fucking, and then, Amber.

"Hey, Brody, listen." Nicco lingered in the bathroom doorway. Their voices echoed in the empty rooms and bounced around inside his newly aching head. He wanted to scream or to climb up on the balcony and make that final swan dive to silence it. Violent tremors gripped his body. His face was hot and wet with tears.

Why was this happening?

Who was he?

Why couldn't he remember?

"That boy, Sam. Sophie's son," he said, his voice hoarse.

"Yours. And so help me, if you tell her I told you I will slice off that giant piece of meat between your legs and serve it to you with fava beans and a nice Chianti," Nicco said. His face split in a grin that seemed so strange and out of place at that moment, Brody laughed. It hurt his chest, but he couldn't stop.

"What you do with this information is up to you." Nicco helped him to his feet. "I'm not here to talk you out of marriage or leaving or anything. But I owe this to you. I swear, I'm so goddamned sorry. Because I consider you more than a teammate, you know?" He stuck out a hand. Brody shook it. "You're a good friend. And you truly got the shit end of this deal."

Brody blinked rapidly, unable to process. He remained still, staring out the window for a long time after Nicco left, taking in the suburban landscape view from his condo without seeing anything.

Chapter Eleven

Sophie looked at the man across from her, listened to him make small talk, and acknowledged she really should be more polite. She ought to at least act like she wanted to be on this date. Smiling, she sipped her wine and attempted to recall what he'd said, if he'd asked her a question or something to prompt the expectant expression on his face.

Susan had fixed her up with him, an emergency room doctor, or something similarly exciting. Handsome, charming, all the things she should want, the guy bored her to tears. Her brain spun and wouldn't let her rest. Coming into her life on the heels of the Brody separation, the poor guy at the table didn't have a chance.

"Um, sorry," she said, reaching for her buzzing phone, figuring Sam had some kind of question for her, trying to distract her in his little boy way from the fact that she wasn't at home with him on a Friday night.

A strange number, without a contact attached, lit the screen. She shoved it back in her purse, letting it go to voicemail. The man continued talking, she continued sipping, picking at her salad and ignoring the fact that not only did her son turn four the next day, Brody would be getting married. She tried not to glance at her phone and wished she were home with Sam, eating popcorn and watching a movie. She had no energy for this dating thing.

The man drove her home and walked her to her door. "Hey." He tilted her chin up, surprising her. "Thanks. I know this was a blind date set up." He raised an eyebrow as if questioning her.

She thought for a half second about how much a nice hard fuck would help right then. But it seemed too much trouble to engineer, even with a guy as handsome and fabulous as the one pressing a soft goodnight kiss to her cheek.

Ducking inside, she shut the door and leaned her forehead against its cool surface. The quiet house calmed her. Sam's cat wound around her ankles. The fridge buzzed, the dryer dinged. All the normal sounds, she thought. No big deal. Just her life, moving on with itself, whether she liked it or not.

She poured a glass of water, looking out over her dark front lawn as she drank it. She'd alerted Dante to her new reality. He'd been understanding, and they were drawing up contracts to alter their ownership arrangement. Part of her didn't want to let it go. She was Katrina, and that persona had provided her with the impetus to recover not only emotionally but financially from the ruin Frank had left with her.

Her phone buzzed again. She pulled it out of her bag, noting the same mystery number. Figuring it might be some random disaster heralded by a media call, she answered. "Hello. This is Sophie Harrison," she said, yawning and leaning against the kitchen counter.

"Hi. It's Brody." His warm, honeyed accent coiled in her consciousness, circled around and settled in a familiar, warm crevice.

"What can I do for you?" She tried to keep it businesslike.

"You in there? I mean, is that you at the kitchen window?" he asked. She turned and peered out, not seeing anything, until his motorcycle headlights flashed.

"What do you want?" She walked to the door and stepped onto the porch, shutting the door behind her. She wouldn't let him into her house. No way.

He wandered up, dressed in suit pants and a dress shirt unbuttoned at the neck. He stayed back from her, loose-limbed, hands in his pockets, a small smile playing over his lips. She frowned at him as she dropped into a seat, gesturing for him to join her.

"I just wanted to say thanks," he said as he perched on the edge of a chair like a cat in a room full of rocking chairs. As if he might bolt off the porch and down the sidewalk in a heartbeat.

"For what?" she asked, using everything she had to not touch him. To beg him to remember her.

"For not telling me." He leaned back, seemingly at ease all of a sudden.

Curious, but with a lick of fear at the base of her brain where Amber's threat still lurked, she stayed quiet. She didn't want to be named the new general manager and then face something like that. But more importantly, she refused to expose Sam to it. Not even for Brody.

"Okay. You're welcome." She got up. "You should go."

"Wait." He held out his hand, palm up.

Tears formed and fell, despite her efforts. It was so Brody, that simple gesture. It killed her because it had started everything for them.

"Don't," she croaked, crossing her arms to keep from falling into him. "Please."

He rose, still with hand outstretched. His eyes were pleading. "I don't remember much. But I know we were together. And I'm glad. I don't mean to upset you, honestly. I just need someone...." His voice broke.

The unbreachable expanse of her small front porch yawned between them. She simply refused to do this. Not as long as Amber made threats with her jealous bullshit. It wasn't worth it.

"You have someone. A wife. Tomorrow."

He sucked in a breath, his face a mask of unhappiness as his arm dropped to his side. It nearly killed her, and she had a brief moment of wonder that her heart could pound so hard and still function. The moment had arrived. Let him back in and risk losing her son forever.

That was no contest.

"Good luck to you, Robert." He winced, blinked fast, then his new Brody face slipped into place. She took a deep breath, relieved and destroyed all in one second.

"Thanks. Take care. Of yourself and him."

She nodded. He turned and walked back down to his bike. She ached where he hadn't touched her. Her arms hurt where she hadn't embraced him. But it had to be this way.

When she opened the door and stepped inside, she very nearly fell right over Sam. Clad in his PJs, clutching his blanket, just a little boy, but with the mature expression of a man, studying her, worry making his brow wrinkly.

"Mommy."

She dropped down to the floor and gathered him in.

"Mommy," he repeated. "Is that soccer man my daddy? The one who saw me, and how great I was, and left us?"

"Yes, Sam, he is. He got sick. He hurt his head really bad. All his memories are gone. He didn't leave you. He never knew about you."

Sam pulled away from her and seemed to puzzle over this, turning it around in his brain. "He doesn't know about me?"

"Yes, baby. I'm sorry," she said, never meaning it more.

"Well, maybe we can give him some medicine. And we can play soccer together. And you guys can make dinner in the kitchen. And we can help him know me." His face, so earnest and full of hope, eviscerated her. She hated herself and Brody for putting this innocent little boy through so much crap.

"No. He's moving away tomorrow."

"On my birthday?" The boy seemed utterly shocked by that. His face fell, a clear sign of oncoming tears.

"Yeah, now let's get some sleep. We have a huge party to get ready for, right?" She tried to stay chipper, to distract him.

But Sam was already crying, full-on sobbing in a way that wasn't a mere temper tantrum. Sophie stood, unable to move for a few minutes when the realization that she had just broken her own son's heart hit her in the gut.

Sick of lying to everyone, furious with herself, she carried him to bed. The sobs reduced to hiccups, then deep breathing as he dropped into his usual tossing-turning sleep cycle. She'd be dealing with this tomorrow for sure. But for now all she managed to do was drop onto her side in his bed and hang onto Sam's warm body like it was the only thing anchoring her to the universe.

Chapter Twelve

The day dawned inauspiciously. Brody had a killer hangover, having gone straight from Sophie's house to a bar. Nicco had picked him up well after two a.m., thanks to a call from the manager, and dropped him at Amber's place since his was now completely empty. He'd woken up with a mouth full of cotton and a pounding, sick headache.

His wedding day, he mused, glaring into the mirror at his bloodshot eyes. It meant little to him. Less than that, really. But he'd set himself on this path and had no idea how to alter it.

The juggernaut of Amber's Wedding Plans had plowed him under. She had a deft hand at involving him enough to keep him mildly interested, yet not so much that he got bored or pissed off by it. The sum total of his responsibility today was represented by the custom-tailored tuxedo hanging in the otherwise empty closet, shined black shoes on the floor beneath.

He downed more water, heartbeat loud in his ears, unable to get the vision of Sophie—so beautiful, so perfect, and so completely, obviously over him or anything they had together—out of his brain. He had to move on. That little boy might be his son. Even if his brain tripped over the word when he acknowledged he had no idea when or how it happened. And if his stupid mind wouldn't allow him to remember enough to make it worth her time? Well, he had to get the fuck over it.

He ran a hand across his rough jaw, tempted not to shave. If for no other reason than to give a real up yours to Amber and her spread-sheeted, over-planned, hyper-organized event because he was a mere player on her stage. Her toy, a plaything, a prop.

He suppressed a rush of nausea. Sophie had rejected him. He had a son whose connection to him would always be as some random guy on the soccer team and no more.

"Fuck!" He pounded the bathroom vanity counter. He didn't want to leave. He didn't want to marry Amber. He'd been grasping at every straw within his immediate reach when she pulled him back from his personal ledge that night. So he'd done the only thing he knew to do by latching onto her and not letting go. *It's not her fault*, he reminded himself, *that you are a giant fucking loser*. And now here he was, hours away from the big event, with nothing between him and honest-to-god misery but an overpriced wedding.

He flipped the switch in his head labeled *wedding autopilot*. Amber had planned an evening nuptial ceremony, thank the Lord, so he got a chance to nap and eat. She wasn't here because part of the plan was for her to be holed up with her posse at some expensive hotel the night before. Around five, he got dressed, stuck his feet in the shoes, leaving his jaw unshaven.

Nicco and Metin picked him up. They handed him a beer. He took it, sipped, winced, and set it down. His stomach churned. He didn't really want to puke all over his friends.

The two men kept quiet. Brody stared out the window, then followed them into the yacht club once they arrived. He'd been there the night before, for the rehearsal, escaping when Amber left with her group of girlfriends. He'd gone to Sophie for reasons he truly didn't understand. He'd hoped to see Sam, truth be told. But she had protected her son, as a mother should.

Before he entered the main hall, greeted by all and knowing no one, Nicco pulled him aside and stuck something in his palm. He stared at the photo in his hand. It was an old one, possibly from that shoebox full of mysteries he'd found in his closet. Sweat broke out on his brow, his body ice cold, quaking, still in the throes of hangover-induced stress.

The image could easily be Sam, the kid he'd met, the boy Nicco claimed he had fathered. A fact Sophie had confirmed before telling him to get out of her house, her life, and away from their son.

He gripped the photo tight, ignoring the surrounding hullabaloo. His vision blurred. His gut churned. Then, without another thought, he started barreling through the crowd, the photo clutched in his fist. Seeking escape in the maze of hallways and doors in the old building where he'd suffered through the rehearsal, where he'd pondered his break away to confront Sophie with Nicco's news flash. Now, however, he wanted nothing whatsoever to do with this farce of an event, with him as central show pony. He would be no one's toy or husbandly arm decoration.

You are my bitch. The voice sliced through his brain. Her voice. The red-headed bitch who'd left him alone ever since he nearly leapt off the balcony and been rescued by Amber London.

Brody. My. Bitch. Her memory screeched in his ear. Get over here and make me come.

He winced and put the fist holding the photo to his forehead, forcing her out and Sophie's deep blue eyes back in.

He shoved open a random door, sucking in huge breaths of fresh spring Michigan air, heart light for the first time in what felt like forever. If he believed Nicco, he, Brody, had once been a very different man. Still the star goalkeeper, independent, stoic, quiet. But deeply in love. And not with scary Amber but with the smart, beautiful Sophie.

Someone grabbed his arm. He tried to yank it away, speechless with his intent to get the hell out before it was too late. Metin stood there, dressed in his own monkey suit, his long, dark hair smoothed back, his hand on Brody's arm in a death grip.

"Where are you going?" he asked, mildly.

"Away from here," Brody blurted out, his brain sending him a single message: Escape. Go to Sophie. Hurry!

"Good plan," Metin said, patting his shoulder. "I'll tell her. I've been dying to pop that bitch's bubble."

Brody grinned, tugged his bowtie loose, and glanced around. He had no real means of escape. Metin turned him and pointed over his shoulder. His bike sat crouched at the curb, metal shining like a beacon.

"Nice." He faced his coach, or rather, his friend. "Thanks."

"Go to her. Make it right. Don't rush her, though. Get to know your son first and prove you're worthy of being a father. It's an honor and something that must be earned. She will judge you by that, not how eager you are to get back into her bed."

He nodded, taking it on, internalizing it, but dying to get away.

But Metin didn't let go of his arm. "Don't fuck this up, Vaughn. Your woman is about to be named general manager of the club. She's going to be the big boss, big time."

Brody blinked. His woman? His? A thrill of possessive lust shot through him at the thought. He took a breath then blew it out, words failing him. Finally, he croaked out. "I just need to see her."

"I know." Metin clapped him on the back again. "Go. I'll tell Amber she's been left at the altar."

"I don't wanna be that guy." He meant it. "Really. I...."

Metin shook his head. "It's no less than she deserves. Trust me."

Taking his keys from Metin's outstretched hand, he headed for the bike, focused on a single goal.

• • • •

AFTER PULLING UP TO Sophie and Sam's house, he turned off the engine and tucked his helmet away. The small front lawn looked like a birthday party war zone, spent water balloons, streamers, and empty cups with soccer balls on them littering its expanse. A huge, Happy Birthday Sam banner hung crookedly across the porch. But no cars lined the streets. All seemed quiet.

He glanced at his watch. If things had gone to plan, he'd be staring down the aisle right then at Amber, future wife, future ex-agent. She'd wanted a classy evening wedding, so by the time he'd bolted the scene and ridden out to Ann Arbor it was nearly eight o'clock. His nerves did an annoying tap dance as he walked up to the front door.

After a couple of knocks and still no answer, he decided to try around back. The deck was worse than the front yard, covered in ripped wrapping paper, more balloons, decorations, food plates. A few tiki torches were spluttering away. A fire blazed in a small outdoor pit. He tiptoed around, not wanting to scare anyone.

Then he spotted them. Sam was sound asleep, flopped against his mother's torso. Sophie's huge blue eyes looked exhausted. He took his time, watching her, drinking her in, wondering how he would possibly fix this, but more determined than ever to do so.

"What are you doing here?" she asked, startling him but not sounding terribly surprised. "Shouldn't you be slipping on a ring, declaring 'til death do you part and all that?" She continued to stare at the fire.

He took a seat next to her, elbows on his knees, the photo of himself still in one hand. "Yeah, well, that didn't work out the way she wanted, I guess."

Sophie turned to him, something like fear on her face. "You have to go back. Marry her. It's best for you both."

"How would you know what's best for me?" he asked, honestly curious. Now that he was here with her, it seemed as though all his troubles—the headaches, sleepless nights, general low-lying frustration—would all vanish into thin air.

"You can't be here. I mean it." She got up, patting Sam's back. The boy snuffled around, rousing enough to spot Brody. He frowned and glanced at his mother, as if seeking something from her. "It's okay, baby," she said. "Brody was just leaving."

"No, actually I'm not." He rose and faced her, pulse racing but never more sure of anything. Sam kept his arm around his mother's neck, but met Brody's eyes. "Here, Sam. I brought this for you." He held out the photo.

Sam took it. "When did you take this picture of me?" he asked, his face covered in a film of icing and dirt. Brody wiped some of the blue and green sugar off his son's cheek. His gut flamed hot with resolve. He wanted this so badly he could taste it on his tongue. Could feel it, deep in his soul.

"It's not of you, honey," Sophie told the boy.

"Your mom is right. It's of me," he said. Sam grinned and before either of them had a chance to react, he reached across the distance between the two adults. Sophie let him go, putting her hand to her lips as her son wrapped his warm body around Brody's torso, burying his face in his father's neck.

"I knew you'd come back," he muttered.

Chapter Thirteen

Brody put Sam to bed, amusing Sophie with practical reminders to brush his teeth and wash the mess off his face first. They chattered away about how they would play soccer tomorrow, first thing. Sophie allowed herself a thrill of emotion when Sam planted a huge kiss on Brody's cheek and gripped him in a long hug.

This could not be happening. Amber would release that damning fake report, and her son would be exposed to her former life as Domme-for-hire. Sam just loved having a man around. He'd get over it soon enough.

She brought them both a beer and they sat, watching the fire burn itself down to coals. "So," she said, "You deserted the lovely Amber right at the altar, did you?"

"Yes, I did," Brody said, hypnotized by the orange glow of the waning fire. Then he grabbed her arm and yanked her close so fast she yelped in surprise. He ran a finger down her face. His lips hovered over hers. A single most perfect moment, until she broke it. Forcing her mouth into a semblance of a smile, she disentangled, gave his arm a sister-like pat, and stood.

"I still don't think you should be here." She walked on wobbly legs to where she'd left a couple of large garbage bags, grabbed them, and shoved one at him. "Here, make yourself useful and help me clean up this chaos."

He stared at the black plastic bag as if she had handed him a live rat. "But," he protested. "I'm...here to...."

She whirled on him, fury clouding her vision. "Your fiancée threatened me, Brody. Threatened my son." She shut her eyes for a split second at the surprise on the man's face as he rose to his feet. "No, no, it's more complicated than you think." In her space now, his very presence forcing the crazed spinning of her brain to settle, he gripped her arms tight, disbelief and fury on his face.

Clutching the garbage bag so tightly it hurt, she stayed focused on what mattered—her son and his well-being. "Don't touch me. Just listen." She didn't trust herself. Because her Robert was back and he wanted to kiss her and god help her, she wanted to let him. And that was out of the question. "Sit." She shoved him down on a lounge chair and took a seat opposite. "I own a business, a different business. It has something to do with your history that you don't remember."

He nodded, his face grim. "Headaches. I get them bad now and I don't know why. And I dream about... I mean, I constantly see and hear this red headed woman, even when I'm awake. She's dressed in leather, and calling me a pussy, and her bitch, and her toy. It hurts. She's hurting me." He ran a hand around the back of his neck. "I think I like it. I mean, I know I do, up to a point. Until she won't let me, um, you know, finish." A flush rose in his cheeks, and Sophie suppressed a smile. "Then she keeps calling me names and shit." His tightly clenched fists rested on his knees. A familiar sign of the frustration she recalled before his collapse over four years ago.

Biting back the urge to soothe with her lips, she settled for touching one of his hands. He had to deal with this on his own. She had no part of him and his life now, nor would she. Her heart could not spare him another moment of consideration. So she kept her touch neutral, and slowly his fist released.

"Yes. You spent almost three years as a submissive. More like a slave, I guess, to one of your professors at Vanderbilt. That's where you went to college and played soccer. Your team won the NCAA championship your senior year." She bit her lip. Doctors, and even her friend Susan, had warned her not to do this. Not to provide memories for him. It wouldn't matter and might make his life worse, knowing things about his life that he had no reference for and likely never would.

"But Brody, you have to know that she was a bad person. I mean, some people do engage in the sort of relationship she pretended to have with you, but she was an abuser. I know it's hard to get right now."

"What else? What about before that? Why do I sometimes see strange women smoking cigarettes and telling me to get my own supper?"

"You were an orphan. Your mom was a drug addict found dead in your house when you were seven or eight and you spent ten years in foster care before you graduated from high school. Then you went to Vandy. When you were a sophomore you met...." She stopped.

She didn't know the woman's name. The woman whose very eyeballs she would merrily rip out of her head for her horrific treatment of the man sitting in front of her now. That nameless woman had damaged his soul, and Sophie would never forgive her for it.

"You started what amounted to a master and slave relationship with a professor. She picked up on the fact that you enjoyed getting off from pain. There's nothing strange about that. Lots of people do. I do, sometimes. But it got you into trouble. Got me into trouble too, thinking that my abuser was someone who cared about me."

He blinked, then his face flushed red again. "Someone hurt you?" He practically growled as he reached for her hand. Her skin pebbled at the sound. The natural connection they shared was so real at that moment, she could see it shimmering, like a cord stretching between them.

"Yes. He nearly killed me. Stole my money. Ran me into debt. He came back, right before we..." She sucked in a breath, did not want to relive this, not now. "You caught him in my office, threatening me. You nearly pounded him into the floor, which was great." She pulled her arm out of his grasp. "He's in jail." She marveled even now at how far she had come since falling into Frank's trap.

"How did we meet? I mean when...we...you know." He blushed like a schoolboy again.

"We met in my office, when you signed your first contract four seasons ago. Rafe had plucked you off some team where you were languishing as a back-up keeper, I forget where. So there you were, signing day, my second season with the Black Jacks. I was overwhelmed, desperate, scared of screwing up, at my first real job since Frank and all that mess."

"You said you had another business." His low voice rumbled around in her brain, reminding her of different, more intimate words in his honey smooth, familiar accent.

"Yes. I was Madame Katrina."

Brody tilted his head, looking confused.

"A Dominatrix-for-hire. I did very well at it. I have a business partner named Dante. He handles security and screening. You were a client once. I mean, you showed up out of the blue, calling yourself Robert." It was Sophie's turn to blush when Brody's eyes darkened, and he leaned closer to her.

"You called me that before," he said. "I know it's the name on my driver's license, but no one ever uses it."

"Except me. Because you were Robert for me that night. You are Robert. You always will be to me."

He started pacing, rubbing the bridge of his nose with thumb and forefinger. She stayed in her seat, wanting to help, upset at making him anxious with her info dump. But she had to do it because he deserved to know why they would never be together. Not as long as Amber lurked around the edges with her fake, yet damning, report.

"We played that night. Sort of. It was one of the most intense encounters I'd ever had." She startled when he whirled to face her, fury on his face.

"Then what? We just jumped into the sack? I knocked you up? What?" His voice, harsh and angry, didn't surprise her.

"No." She rose and started scooping birthday-cake-encrusted paper plates into the garbage bag. "No," she whispered again, reliving her rejection of him, his repeated attempts to get her to go out on a date. "We sort of flirted, I guess, for a while. Texting, emails, internet chats while you were gone on road trips with the team. You asked me out on dates. I wouldn't go."

His face lost some of its angry tightness at that. "Somehow, that doesn't surprise me."

She sighed, intimidated at how much actual mess there was to clean up and sat back down, giving up for the moment. "Then Frank showed up. My 'bad guy.'" She hooked her fingers around the words but got a chill recalling that day. "He came to my office after some money he'd been hiding in my house, money he stole from me. He got physical. You burst into my office with security and manhandled him. So I owed you. So we went out. Well, actually, we never made it out of my house that night."

He smiled. Her heart soared at the sight of it, and the memory she'd not allowed herself to revisit of that incredible night. It had been difficult, painful in a way, but they'd purged something between them. "It was great. That night." She was unable to stop the tear from sliding down her cheek. He touched it. Put his finger to his lips.

"But you had a concussion. You shouldn't have been playing."

"Yeah, Nicco told me that." He heaved a sigh.

Her heart pounded. "What else did Nicco tell you?"

"He told me not to tell you he did but he came to my packed-up condo and told me about you, and me, and about Sam, because he wanted me to not fuck up, to not marry Amber. And because he blamed himself." Brody touched his head, his face confused and unhappy again. "Goddamn it. I can't remember any of this."

Without thinking, she reached out to touch his rough face. In a flash, he grabbed her and before she knew it had her pulled onto his lounge chair, his mouth on hers, urgent, seeking, both of them making noises of protest while tugging at clothes.

All she wanted in her life, she had, right now, in her arms. The lonely, sleepless nights, missing him, wanting his help with Sam, with a major decision she had to make about her career. Everything was so damn overwhelming right now.

"Oh," she said when his lips slid down her neck, hitting all her sweet spots. "I think you remember some things." He tugged her t-shirt up and off, tugged down her jeans and had her naked within seconds. She paused, then did the same to him, their breathing loud in her ears.

"Please," he whispered into her skin, pulling her until they lay side-by-side on the lounge chair. "Sophie, I need you so much."

"Shh..." She held him close. They were shielded from neighbor view by the oversized umbrella that shaded the deck, but suddenly she didn't care who saw or heard her cries of delight. His warm flesh was so familiar to her, his body so full of memory. She shifted her hips, took him inside her. He thrust deep, pulling her down to meet his lips.

"Robert," she whispered, fighting back tears. The orgasm hit her hard as he gripped her hips and stared at her while she let it roll through and over her, wave after wave of pleasure.

She smiled down at him, then lowered her mouth to his nipple, sucking and biting as she tightened her body around him. "Come," she muttered into his skin. "I need to feel it."

He groaned, obviously trying to stop himself. She raised her face from his chest and placed her palms on his firm torso. "No holding back, Robert." She rolled her hips, anticipating what the new angle and change of friction would do for him. He cried out so loudly, she covered his mouth with her palm, and rode him, having another little spasm of pleasure at the warm sensation of his climax inside her.

She draped down over him, both of them still half-dressed, their breathing calming. She spoke into his neck, needing him to know all of it.

"Amber found out about the Madame Katrina thing somehow. It's now a more organized dating service, a specialized one, for people who require a little more than the usual," she said, then climbed off him, taking a seat on the lounge chair next to his legs. He lay still, one arm propped behind his head, gazing at her.

"What I do is not technically against the law. At least not the way I have the business structured for government purposes. I pay my taxes, report my employees. I even offer them insurance. If, at the end of the date, there is sex, money isn't exchanged, not that night." She shrugged. "Anyway, somehow Amber found out. Showed up at my office accusing me of running a prostitution ring and saying she had to report me to child protective services." She shivered, wanting Brody's arms around her again. He zipped up his tuxedo trousers, then helped her back into her clothes, before sitting and putting his arm around her shoulders.

"I won't let her do anything like that, I promise."

"It's probably too late. She knows you would come to me. She knows Sam is yours. You were too busy the last three years fucking your way through Detroit socialites, then getting sucked into her circle, to notice the kid right under your nose who was like a Brody mini-me." She jumped up, rubbing her elbows, already regretting this whole thing.

He frowned and stood, tried to hang onto her, but she wrenched away, furious for being weak and giving in to her base need for him, again. Terror washed over her. The woman had probably already leaked her stupid report. It would be all over the news any minute.

"Shit," she spat out, already wondering how she could spin it.

"I have a few things on Amber she won't want revealed. Let me handle it."

"No, damn it. I don't want to get into a pissing contest with her. She'll win."

"No. She won't. You have to trust me." He grabbed her and folded her into his embrace. She gave in, burying her nose in his chest and wrapping her arms around him. "I'll fix this." They stood together, arms around each other's waists, the night sounds rising around them. "I want to be with you, and with Sam."

She pulled back so she could look straight at him. "I can't let you all the way back into my life. Not yet. I will let you get to know your son. He's getting to the point where he needs his father. So this works." She was already compartmentalizing how she might share Sam, but not her heart. "Although I don't know how we can manage it if you're in Boston."

"I'm not going to Boston." His dark eyes shone. "God, I love kissing you." He tried to do that, but she ducked away.

"Uh, they're expecting you. Paid for you already. Contracts signed, remember?"

"Yeah, but I'm close to the head of legal for my team. I hear she's pretty damn tough. I'll bet she can get me out of it if I work really hard to convince her it's worth it." He grinned and slid his hands down her back to cup her ass. "I'm a hard worker."

He did kiss her then, and she did nothing to stop him, gasping when he managed to bring her to the knife edge of another orgasm within minutes, shoved up against the outside wall of her house, his lips on hers, his hand down the front of her jeans.

"This is not going slow." She sighed and let it happen, anyway.

"I'm not going anywhere, not anymore. You can't make me." He grinned. "Let's just have another little reunion moment, shall we?" He pulled her palm down to his zipper. "Turn around," he whispered. "Put your hands on the wall."

She did and the sensation of him inside her once more never felt more perfect. He gathered her close at the last moment, filling her ears with his sounds of pleasure. "I don't remember much. But I am game to make some new memories," he said, his voice low and hoarse.

Stupid girlie tears of relief made her sniffle. "I don't know."

"I do know. For once, you're going to listen to me. I won't hurt you, I promise, but you have to trust me. I'll fix the thing with Amber." Sliding his hand up to her throat, he held just tight enough to turn her on all over again. "I will get to know our son." His hips moved, thrusting, rolling, their bodies staying connected. “I will get to know you again.”

“Yes,” she said, smiling and reaching back to clutch his hair.

Epilogue

Brody watched from the porch while the kids rolled around with the puppy he'd brought home, much to Sophie's displeasure. He smiled, shaking his head at the coffee cup she offered him, tugging her down into his lap for a kiss instead.

"I told you, no dogs," she said into his lips.

"I'll make it up to you." He cupped her bare breast under her sweatshirt.

"Cut it out." She smacked his hand away when their sons bounded up the steps and barreled past them into the house.

The year they'd spent after that night on the deck of Sam's birthday had been tough. She'd rebuffed him emotionally after convincing Jack to take the monetary hit and buy him back for the team.

Of course, Sam fell head over heels for his dad, and by the time he turned five, the two of them had concocted an elaborate treasure hunt for her that took her all around the neighborhood with hints and prizes. When she found the final prize, and had the small ring box in her hand, her first inclination was to scoff and remind Brody she had no intention of getting married, to anyone, ever.

But as she stood near the back shed, her fingers covered in dirt where she'd had to dig around to find the damn thing, she saw Brody kicking the soccer ball around with Sam, keeping an eye on her, his face neutral. She'd nodded and Brody had said something to Sam, who then came running at her, yelping with delight.

"Under one condition," she said later, as her man held her close, the adult celebrations concluded.

"Anything," he gasped, trying to catch his breath.

She sat up. "You retire." She frowned down at his seeming blasé acceptance of her words. "I mean it. Your headaches are back again. I'm not going to marry you, make us a family, and then lose you to this stupid game. You stay home, consult, coach, I don't give a shit. I make plenty of money and you have plenty saved. I want us to be happy for a long time. No more pro goalie play. It's the only way I will agree to this."

"Hmmm..." He stretched. And her mouth watered at the sight of his sexy, tattooed torso. "If I'm staying at home, I might get bored."

"Just text me and I'll rush home to alleviate boredom." She'd settled back into his arms, content.

"Then it's a deal."

And now, she sat in her husband's lap, enjoying the morning, and reflecting on her luck. They had agreed they wanted more kids. But also that she shouldn't risk another pregnancy. Given his background, it made sense for them to find kids who needed good homes.

So they had three sons now. Allen was almost Sam's age, a shy, but sweet boy, whose single mother had ended up in prison for cooking meth in his bedroom. Tommy was a two-year old who got placed with them within weeks of welcoming Allen to their family, which made for some pretty crazy days and nights as they assimilated into their new configuration.

Tommy had come to them with his arm in a cast from a fall and horrible burn marks on his forehead from his time at a foster home. Brody had heard about it one morning from their attorney and had her in front of him to sign papers by afternoon. She still wasn't quite sure taking on another boy would be a good idea, and so soon after adding Allen to the family.

But he had the whole thing in control, the boys, the house, everything. She was general manager for the Black Jacks and had overseen four years of up and down seasons, but mostly success. Her sons were five, ten, and eleven. She loved her husband, but for that damn dog, whining now because he couldn't get up the steps to follow the boys into the house.

Brody consulted with Rafe and handled recruiting for the team for a while until the adoptions started coming through. Now, a self-proclaimed Mrs. Dad—as opposed to Mr. Mom, which he didn't like—he handled almost everything related to their home life. They'd hired someone to help with laundry and housecleaning which left him free to concoct meals, field trips, and outings, generally being the father he'd never had.

He managed boys all day long, from morning to night, and planned to start coaching as soon as Tommy started school. The Amber thing had gone away, just like he promised. She'd done some shady things with several of her male clients, many of them performance-enhancing drug-related, which Brody had found out when she'd tried to get him to visit one of the innocuous clinics in Florida. Turned out her concern about her rep and career overshadowed her desire to be Mrs. Vaughn.

"How did I get here? With you?" Sophie sighed, curling up in his lap as a minor world war brewed in the house behind them.

"Luck." He kissed her. "Karma," he muttered around her lips.

"All the above."

"Hop up, Soph." He pushed her off his lap. "Sounds like my presence as a referee is required inside."

"Thank you," she said, dropping into the chair he'd vacated.

He cupped her chin. "No, thank you."

• • • •

THE END

Well now that we know Sophie's going to be in charge while Brody's home with the kids, let's find ourselves a new player to obsess over. How about DECLAN, the hot Scot just added to the team as forward?

Check out this sneak peek at HAT TRICK...

It was a match like any other. The crowd roared. The heat baked his skin. He heard nothing but the breathing of the defenders—the men he had to break through to get to the goal, *his* goal, to winning the game. Because that was what he got paid to do—win soccer games.

Never mind they were playing some kind of lame-ass friendly, preseason crap.

"BJs! BJs! BJs!" the raucous fans chanted, having latched onto the shorthand version of their team name—the Black Jacks—in a way that fit, considering what a soap opera of an outfit it had turned out to be. He blocked the noise, set his jaw, and kept moving through the thin wall of protection, planting the ball in the upper left corner of the net, giving the flat-footed goalkeeper a little salute and a smile as he jogged past him.

Too bloody easy.

His teammates joined him in a scrum near the edge of the pitch, already celebrating the now-guaranteed victory over the Pittsburgh Arseholes or whatever they were called. Declan didn't know or care. He accepted the kudos, trotted to the middle of the field so the arseholes could start over, and immediately snagged the ball from one of them and played keep-away for the final five minutes of the match.

Game over.

Detroit Black Jacks: 2.

Pittsburgh Arseholes: 1.

Not that it mattered.

"De*clan*! De*clan*! De*clan*!" The crowd had a new cry now, and one that made his face hot. No matter how famous he might have been at one time, he never adjusted to being the center of attention, especially since that, in turn, brought on a distinctly female squeal of embarrassingly loud delight. He whipped off his uniform jersey, a stupid ploy the team's marketing geniuses had forced on the players. It earned them endless internet press for being the *Expansion Team With The Most Naked Flesh* award or some other important designation.

Whatever sold tickets.

After wiping his streaming face with the jersey, he heaved it into an apoplectic crowd of fans—mostly girls.

It was a buzz, he'd give it that.

He smiled, the nearly perpetual blush still warming his face. How they built the cost of all those new uniform shirts into the team's budget, he had no idea. Seemed like a waste to him, but he was a tightwad Scot as his teammates liked to remind him, usually after he'd passed on yet another opportunity to throw his hard-earned cash onto a poker table or tuck it into a stripper's G-string.

• • • •

DECLAN GLARED AT HIS friend and teammate across the hood of the car. "You know I don't like to—"

Jason climbed behind the wheel of his Shelby Mustang, a royal blue monstrosity of Detroit rolling iron, and fired up the engine, cutting off his sentence. Declan trudged around to the passenger's side and dropped into the soft black leather seat. "I don't like these clubs, you know that. I—I had plans for tonight. I'm...I was..." He gripped the dashboard when Jason peeled out of the garage.

"You are a lame, tight-fisted, boring motherfucker and I have taken it upon myself to get you laid, hard. Maybe more than once." Jason glanced at him as they idled at a stoplight. Declan frowned at him. "No, don't thank me yet. I'm sick and tired of you wasting all your God-given goods sitting around and counting your money or whatever the hell it is you do when we aren't practicing or playing."

Declan blew out a breath, determined not to argue since it would be fruitless. He *did* have a life. He liked his routines and he was perfectly happy. Declan MacGuire didn't do nightclubs, strip joints, one-night stands, or groupies.

Not that he didn't have ample opportunity to try them all.

His mystery man persona only seemed to make the @DecMac Ginger Lover Brigade on Twitter louder and more determined to do exactly what his friend on the team had stated he would do tonight. His scalp tingled in spite of himself. He hadn't gotten laid in a damn long time.

He'd left that life behind, including the woman he'd loved when he'd moved here, determined to focus on his career. He left romance for the saps and losers.

"My goal-scoring friend, you are gonna get your ginger world rocked tonight." Jason laughed and screeched away from the intersection.

Deciding that silence was the best option, Declan stayed that way. By the time he and Jason entered the penthouse nightclub in some random Detroit suburb, he'd resigned himself to tolerate the party experience, have a couple of drinks, and get the hell home.

He was on his second beer when he saw her, or more precisely, her hair. The gold satin curtain of it hid half her face as she sipped some kind of pink colored drink through a straw. Her bright red lips puckered just enough to make the skin on the back of Declan's neck prickle. She looked bored sitting next to some other girl he hardly registered. A drop of sweat formed on his temple, but he had frozen in place—pinned to his spot by the woman's eyes, which met his the instant before he looked away.

She blinked slowly, as if processing him and his gawping stare. Something alarming clambered up his spine and into his brain. She smiled at him, a pleasant enough smile, if a little crooked, he thought as he perused her other features.

After avoiding her most of the night, he finally worked up the nerve to walk over to her. He tried to look casual about it but could sense every eyeball in the place staring at him as he made his way through the crowd towards the beautiful woman. The split second he close enough to reach out and touch her arm, a large, man-shaped torpedo shot past him and scooped the object of his newfound obsession up and into his arms. She squealed in pretend indignation, then, to Declan's unsurprised disappointment, wrapped herself around the guy and kissed him like someone was paying her to make it look good.

He sighed and leaned one elbow on the bar. When the hot chick bartender raised an eyebrow at him he nodded and a fresh beer appeared at his elbow.

"That's me, love. A day late, a pound short," he said, raising his pint to the woman behind the bar. She licked her lips and raised that eyebrow again. "Thanks. But no thanks." He downed the brew, clapped the empty on the bar and headed for the door.

• • • •

HAT TRICK IS A FRIENDS to lovers, fake relationship, sunny/grumpy rom com that will have you laughing and cheering for all the characters!

NOW you really should dive into the series that started it all, The Stewart Realty Series!

It is best enjoyed in this order:

Floor Time

Sweat Equity

Closing Costs

Dual Agency

Escalation Clause

Conditional Offer

Mutual Release

Backup Offer

Good Faith (This novel is not a romance but a 2nd generation novel with plenty of romantic elements. Please read the content warnings before you start).

About Liz Crowe

• • • •

LIZ CROWE IS A KENTUCKY native and graduate of the University of Louisville living in South Carolina. She's spent her time as a three-continent expat trailing spouse, mom of three, real estate agent, brewery owner and bar manager, and is currently a digital marketing and fundraising consultant, in addition to being an award-winning author.

The Liz Crowe backlist has something for any reader seeking complex storylines with humor and complete casts of characters that will delight and linger in the imagination long after the book is finished.

Her favorite things to do when she's not scrolling social media for cute animal videos is walk her dogs, cuddle her cats, and watch her favorite sports teams while scrolling social media for cute animal videos.

Follow along with Liz online at lizcrowe.com

Sign up for her newsletter at lizcrowe.com

Follow/ like @lizcroweauthor on Facebook, Instagram, Twitter, TikTok

Milton Keynes UK
Ingram Content Group UK Ltd.
UKHW020905140524
442690UK00014B/474